Wild Daisies

An Appalachia-Inspired Short Story Collection

Jan-Carol
Publishing, Inc
"every story needs a book"

Wild Daisies
An Appalachia-Inspired
Short Story Collection

Published May 2018
Mountain Girl Press
Imprint of Jan-Carol Publishing, Inc
Copyright © 2018 Wild Daisies

ISBN: 978-1-945619-59-5
Library of Congress Control Number: 2018944917

You may contact the publisher:
Jan-Carol Publishing, Inc.
PO Box 701
Johnson City, TN 37605
publisher@jancarolpublishing.com
jancarolpublishing.com

This is dedicated to all the talented authors for their participation in this collection of short stories, and to all the readers of Jan-Carol Publishing's books.

Table of Contents

Right or Wrong   1
Jan Howery

Set Up   9
Linda Hudson Hoagland

Second Chances   19
Victoria Fletcher

Gumption   23
Lori C. Byington

Just Drive   29
Linda Hudson Hoagland

Bess's Story   37
Julia Parsell

Pretty Ribbons   45
Cheryl Livingston

Pounding Footsteps   53
Linda Hudson Hoagland

Sarah-Hannah   61
Betty Kossick

Wild Daisies

Right or Wrong

Jan Howery

April 12, 1861 – May 13, 1865

The Civil War, also known as "The War Between the States," was fought between the United States of America and the Confederate States of America, a collection of eleven southern states that left the Union in 1860 and 1861 and formed their own country in order to protect the institution of slavery.

On Monday, May 9, 1864 — under a beautiful sun-splashed sky in the mountains of southwestern Virginia — the largest Civil War battle ever fought in that sector of the Old Dominion erupted at the base of Cloyds Mountain in Pulaski County. Both Yankee and Rebel veterans of that engagement, many of whom had fought in larger and more important battles elsewhere, claimed the intensity of this battle exceeded them all. Of the roughly 9,000 soldiers engaged, 1,226 became casualties. Union killed, wounded, and missing were approximately 10 percent of their forces, and Confederate losses approached an appalling 23 percent. The next day, May 10, another lovely spring day, Northern and Southern forces clashed again when a fierce two and one-half hour cannon duel broke out about 10 miles east of Cloyds Mountain at Central Depot (now, the city of Radford.) Here, artillerists blazed away from

1

opposite sides of the New River to determine whether the crucial railroad bridge over this ancient stream would survive or be destroyed. Among the Federal combatants who fought at Cloyds Mountain and the New River Bridge were two future presidents of the United States. Perhaps even more intriguingly, a Union cavalryman who fell at the New River proved to be a woman, one of the few females known to have been killed in combat in the entire war.

"Brother against brother" is a slogan used in histories of the American Civil War, describing the predicament faced in families (primarily, but not exclusively, residents of Border States) in which loyalties and military service were divided between the Union and the Confederacy.

The following fictional story is inspired by actual events and actual letters written during the Civil War.

Right or Wrong?

No one spoke as Ma served up breakfast. The silence was deafening. Ma sat at one end of their wooden handmade kitchen table and Pa sat at the other end. Two twin brothers, James and Thomas, sat across from each other at the table, and neither looked up as they grabbed the bacon and gravy and biscuits.

After pouring Pa's coffee, Ma sat down and stared at her plate. Pa took a sip of his coffee and looked at his sons, first to the right at Thomas, then to the left to James. He spoke very clearly, "You two, to have been born on the same day with the same mother and father, ya both are as different as day and night. I just don't understand it."

James and Thomas were not identical twins, and were opposite in many ways. James was tall, with dark eyes and straight dark hair, and was quiet and reserved. Thomas was a small framed young man with piercing blue eyes and brown wavy hair, and had a hot temper. They were different from birth.

"The only thing you two have ever agreed on is that cute little girl across the mountain. Ya both sparked with her. Is this where it all started?" Pa asked and stared at them.

James and Thomas gave each other a blank stare.

"Well, answer me," snapped Pa.

2

"Pa, this has nothing to do with her. I just think that the north is wrong," James answered.

"The north is not wrong! The north will win this war 'cause they're right," yelled Thomas.

"Boys, we don't have a stake in this war. In war, there's not a right or wrong. It's about people dying for somebody else's ideals. These mountains belong to us, and we don't need to get into a war. We don't have slaves, and we do just fine. We take care of our own. We don't need to go fight someone else's fight," Pa said with sternness.

"I've made up my mind, Pa. I am going to join the Confederates. Why, you can even hear gun fire! They're getting close. We can't just sit here and not get involved. The union soldiers are burning farms and destroying our way of life. I am leaving today," James said calmly.

"You do just that! I will see you on the battlefield," yelled Thomas. "Long live the Union! You will die..."

"Stop it! Just stop it," cried Ma. She stood up and walked away crying.

"Sons, look at what this'll do to your Mother! How can you do this? Divide the family? I forbid it!" Pa declared.

"Pa, I'm packed and will be leaving after breakfast," James said.

"Me too, Pa. I'm leavin' and joinin' the union," Thomas said proudly.

For a few minutes, no one spoke. The boys watched Pa. He lost color in his face and became very pale. He sat there as if the wind had been knocked out of him. *My boys, God, my boys,* he thought. *They're only sixteen.*

James spoke up, "Do you want to walk with me to the fork of the road? I go south and cross over Ridge Mountain. I'll be walkin'."

Before Pa could answer, Thomas interjected, "Walk with us both, Pa. I'll go north and cross over Barn Mountain, and I'll be walkin' too."

James stood up and walked out of the room only to return with his bedroll and gun. Thomas did the same and returned with his bedroll and gun, too.

"We're leaving Pa," James said. Ma could be heard crying in the upstairs bedroom.

"Did you say goodbye to Mother," Pa asked with little emotion.

"Yes," James answered.

3

"Yes," Thomas said.

Pa stood up and grabbed his hat and walked out of the kitchen down the hallway to the front door. They followed him.

"Do you have your bibles?" Pa asked.

James and Thomas both nodded yes.

"Go get your horses and we'll ride down to the fork of the road," Pa suggested.

The three of them saddled up the horses and headed to the fork of the road, which was about a mile from their home. The fork in the road was called that because the road came to an end. You either went to the left, over Ridge Mountain, or to the right, over Barn Mountain, but not forward. It was a split between two mountains.

Together, all three dismounted their horses. Pa took the reins of their horses, and looked at both of them and said, "Sons, I'm asking that you do not do this. But, you'll not listen to me. But, as you leave me and leave each other, I want you to hug each other and tell the other one you love 'em."

James and Thomas hesitated and looked at each other. James stepped forward and the brothers embraced. "You're my brother, and I do love ya," James said.

"Me too," Thomas said, and pulled away quickly.

"Please write if you can and let your Ma know how you're doing," Pa said. "And I love you both."

The boys hugged their father, and turned with a waived goodbye. James turned left, going south, and Thomas turned right, going to the north. Pa watched them as they disappeared out of sight across the mountains.

For the next several months, Pa rode into town every Wednesday. At the court house, there was a list of the dead or missing. The list wasn't always updated every Wednesday, but Pa never knew for sure when it would be updated. He rode into town to make sure that he didn't miss any updates. The horseback ride was about a three hour ride one way. Ma would pack a lunch for him, and there was a natural spring along the way that provided water for him and his horse.

When Pa arrived at the court house, he stood in line to view the list. People would crowd and push to get to see the list. He could hear the yelling and crying when a loved would read the name of a dead relative. With his hat in his hand, he would slowly move with heavy steps inching to what he called the 'dead or alive notice.'

Ma would be standing at the door when Pa arrived home, wringing her hands with a fright in her eyes. Pa would give her a slight smile, and she knew that for another week, her sons were still okay.

After several months, a letter arrived. Pa handed the letter to Ma, but she started to cry and handed the letter back to Pa. He opened the letter and read out loud,

Dearest Mother,

I hope that this finds you and Father both doing well.
Will you and Father ever forgive me for joining the Union side?
We must defend our homeland and our way of life.
We have no choice.
We are Virginians first, and Americans second.
My brother James does not feel this way.
He does more thinking than I do.
I follow my heart and my home.
Oh, how I wish we were fighting side by side,
instead of against each other.
I miss him so. God be with him in this awful hour.
After this is over, I want to go home to Virginia.
I hope you will accept me back.
I will finish this letter tomorrow.

Your son,
Thomas

Pa's eyes teared up and his hands trembled. Ma began to cry inconsolably. Pa took her hands and quoted from the Bible, "Remember Matthew 11:28, 'Come to Me, all you who labor and are heavy laden, and I will give you rest.'"

Over the next few weeks, another letter arrived. It was from James.

5

My Dearest Mother and Father,

I hope this letter finds its way to you. As I write, we all fear the battle tomorrow. Still, the men sit around the campfire singing and writing letters.

The younger boys talk about their fears. They fear being separated from the unit; they fear dying alone; they fear not being identified if they die.

A boy sleeping next to me is younger than me. He is 15. Tonight he told me, "As the bullets were flying over me today, I thought what a foolish boy I was to run away from home and get into this mess. I would be glad to see my father come after me now."

He said he marched off with 34 soldiers from his town, and now, only four are still alive. Many young boys joined to escape the boredom of farm life. They expected a good time, an adventure.

Not much talk about glory or honor now. We talk about going home. Who would have thought it would last this long. My thoughts are of home, and of brother Thomas and all we left behind. Forgive me for leaving. I dream of being home again. I hope to continue this letter tomorrow.

Love from your son,
James

Days turned into months and no more letters arrived. But as months turned into seasons, Pa faithfully saddled up and rode to the courthouse each week.

It was a warm April day when Pa arrived in town. The town was filled with yelling people, and the townspeople were dancing in the streets. He jumped off his horse and walked through the crowd. He stopped a stranger and asked, "What's going on here? What's happening?"

The stranger yelled loudly, "The war...the war is over! Over! Lee surrendered! The war's over!"

The war is over? Pa thought. *That means my boys will be coming home!* But the dreaded notice was updated with names of the soldiers who would never return home. Pa pushed his way through the crowd to the courthouse, and the new list was posted. As he read the names, he trembled with fear. *What if?* But as he read the last name, he let out a sigh of relief.

Walking back to his horse, he saw a newspaper on the ground. Crumbled and dirty, he picked it up. The headline read:

"Lee Surrenders; War is Over"

Pa hurried home. He jumped off the horse and ran to Ma, whom was standing at the door. She started to cry, thinking that one of her sons had been killed.

"No! Ma, No! The war's over! The war is over and their names are not on the list! Our boys will be coming home soon! Thank the Lord in heaven, our sons are comin' home!"

Each day passed with the hope of their sons returning home. It was now in the month of June, and there had been no word from the boys. But on this June morning, the sun was shining brightly and there was a new freshness in the air.

Ma was preparing breakfast when Pa walked into the kitchen. She turned and spoke very calmly, "Pa...I had a dream last night. I saw my boys. I saw 'em walking barefoot. They're near. Our boys are comin' home."

"Then I have to do something Ma. I'll take their horses down to the fork of the road and leave 'em there for the boys. I can fetch water and food for 'em, and the horses will be safe. Maybe I should wait for 'em," Pa said waiting for Ma to agree.

"They'll be here today, Pa. I saw it my dream. I believe," Ma said with a smile on her face.

"Now Ma, don't be gettin' your hopes up. You know there were boys...," Pa stopped before he finished his sentence. Since the war ended, he had stopped going to town to read the 'death notices' because he wanted to believe his sons would return.

"Pa, you need to take the horses down to the fork today. I saw it in my dream. I feel it in my heart. A mother knows," Ma said assuredly.

Pa wanted to believe Ma was right. So, he saddled up three horses and headed to the fork of the road. He prayed that his boys would return safely. *Will the boys be full of hatred?* he thought. *They have seen so much death. Will they be hurt? What if they never come home?*

Pa's thoughts were interrupted by the squawking of some birds flying overhead as he arrived at the fork. He sat there staring at the birds, then looked to the left and then to the right. *Divided,* he thought. *Divided and brother against brother.*

He dismounted and as he did, he caught a glimpse of something moving far away on the top of Barn Mountain. He looked. He stared. *Was it a wild animal? Or...could it be?* he thought. *Could it be...my boy?*

"Pa... Pa... Is that you? It's me!" The words echoed loudly between the two mountains. It was Thomas.

Pa stood in shock. Thomas moved as quickly as he could, but he was hurt. "I'm ok, Pa. I'm ok," he yelled. "Pa! I'm comin' home!"

Just as Pa realized it was Thomas, words echoed loudly from the other direction, "Pa! Pa, can ya hear me? Pa! Pa! Can you see me? I'm home Pa!"

Pa looked to the left and saw someone coming across the top of Ridge Mountain. *What! Could it be? My other son? Is it James?*

"Pa! It's James. I'm comin' home!"

Pa was overtaken by joy. Tears flowed down his face like water flowing from a natural spring. His boys were coming home. He fell to knees, praising God.

As the boys neared the fork, Pa could see that Thomas's clothes were tattered, and he had a leg and arm bandaged and was barefoot. James was moving along with a crutch, and he too was barefoot except for a few rags wrapped around his feet. Pa stood up and didn't know which way to turn. He waited as his boys embraced him. The boys hugged their father, crying and sobbing, and asking for forgiveness.

Pa pulled away and looked at them. "We're home Pa," Thomas cried.

Thomas turned to James and said, "I wasn't right."

James replied, "and I was wrong."

As they hugged each other, Pa thought, *No one was right and no one was wrong.*

Set Up

Linda Hudson Hoagland

My trip to the grocery store was uneventful. But, as I turned onto my street, I noticed the police cars surrounding my house.

Should I stop or keep going?

I drove slowly trying to catch a glimpse of what was happening. Neighbors were gathering on the street in front of the house. I saw my friend, Ginger, standing in the center of the crowd.

I drove passed my driveway and pulled into a parking lot at the church. I yanked my cell phone from my handbag and pressed the buttons that would ring Ginger's cell phone.

"What's going on at my house," I asked in a loud whisper after Ginger answered my ring.

"I was told it was a drug raid," she said in a conspiratorial whisper.

"A drug raid? At my house?" I screamed in response, "I don't do drugs!"

"I know – I know, but that's what they are saying," she explained.

"Who is saying that?"

"Annie told me," said Ginger.

"How did Annie know?"

"I don't know. Someone told her, but I don't have any idea who said it," answered Ginger.

"Well, I guess I will turn around and go home. I really want to see

9

what they are looking for in my house," I said with exasperation verging onto tears.

I backed up and situated my vehicle so I could drive off the parking lot. I paused, cast my eyes to the sky, and whispered a prayer for help.

The crowd was getting larger and my driveway was completely blocked by police vehicles of all kinds. I turned my car onto Ginger's driveway, exited, and made my way to the legal official standing in front of the steps that led to my porch.

"You can't go in there," he said sternly when I tried to move passed him.

"Why not," I demanded.

"This is a crime scene," he said back to me.

"I live here. This is my house. It wasn't a crime scene when I left to go to the grocery store. Why are you here?"

"Wait right here, ma'am. I will get the detective for you. He can tell you what you need to know," he said. He turned to enter my house leaving me stand there with my mouth open to say a few more words of anger.

Momentarily he returned with a gentleman clad in a suit and tie, whom looked all official.

"Are you Louella Spencer," asked the suited man.

"Yes, who are you?" I demanded to know in a not too pleasant tone.

"Detective Mason, ma'am. I need to ask you some questions," he said brusquely.

"I need some answers from you, too. Like why are you searching my house? What are you looking for? Or, who are you looking for?" I could feel my face redden from the anger that was surging through me.

"I'm the person who is asking the questions," he said sternly.

"I'm not going to answer anything until you tell me what this is about," I snapped.

"Mrs. Spencer..." he started.

"Ms. Spencer, there is no mister at this time," I interrupted.

"Ms. Spencer, it has come to our attention that there has been some drug trafficking being carried out on the premises. Do you know anything about that?" he asked. He was looking directly into my eyes. I knew he was trying to assess whether or not I was being truthful.

"Drug trafficking? Not in my house! I am a widow. I live alone and I do not sell drugs of any kind," I stammered angrily. My temper was getting out of control. I really wanted to reach out, grab hold of the detective, and shake him until his teeth rattled.

Suddenly a uniformed policeman stepped up next to the detective. The two men exchanged whispers. The detective turned to face me.

"Ms. Spencer, turn around please," he instructed.

"Why?" I asked angrily.

"You are being placed under arrest for drug distribution," he said.

"Hold off on that for a bit. No cuffs yet," said the chief who had entered the room.

Angry tears started rolling down my cheeks that were red from embarrassment along with the anger.

"What drugs? The only drugs I have in my house are my stomach pills and a fluid pill, and both are prescribed. I have over the counter medications. I don't use drugs and I definitely don't sell drugs," I sputtered between sobs.

"Tell it to the judge, ma'am. Anything you say now can be used against you," the detective said.

"I know – I know – I know my rights. I've seen it all on television. I want a lawyer," I cried.

I cast my gaze to a man whom I thought was a friend. "What's going on, Barry?" I asked as I took a deep breath. I was having a difficult time trying to control my tone with Barry Hendricks, Chief of Police of the Town of Stillwell who had been my friend for many years.

"Don't get too excited, Louella. This is all for show, a set-up," he explained.

"Set up? What are you talking about? You are searching my house and that's for show? A set up, for whom?" I sputtered.

"Yes, it's a set up but we aren't after you for anything. Just listen, okay?" he said calmly.

"This had better be good," I said harshly but with some of the anger draining my body, leaving me a bit weak.

"What do you know about Ginger Hampton?" he asked.

"Ginger is my neighbor and friend. I have known her since I moved here a couple of years ago. She doesn't sell drugs, does she?" I asked.

11

"We have it on good authority that she does exactly that," Barry said.

"She has never said anything to me about drug dealing," I said in a deflated tone. "She does have a lot of company but I thought they were friends of her kids whom were running in and out of the house," I explained.

"How many children does Ginger Hampton have," Barry asked.

"Two boys and a girl, all teenagers," I answered.

"Do they all use the Hampton name?"

"No, Ginger said she was married three times, and they each had different fathers. That seemed odd to me because their ages are so close together. She also said she went back to using her maiden name. So — they all have different names," I said defensively.

"Ginger Hampton has never been married and has never had any children according to the records we have searched. Would you be able to identify some the children and/or visitors," asked Barry.

"Yes, but won't that get me into hot water? Drug dealers are not nice people, except for Ginger. I always thought she was so nice. I guess I was wrong," I said softly.

"She had a lot of people fooled, Louella," said Barry.

"What is arresting me supposed to prove?"

"It gives us a reason to do more investigating without your neighbors being aware," he explained.

"How do you figure that? Won't they, the buyers, steer clear of the place with the cops next door," I asked in astonishment.

"Yes, that could happen. But — they might think this is the best thing that could happen. They could sell their drugs without any fear of getting caught because the legal authorities are investigating you, not them," he explained further.

"My neighbors are going to think I'm a drug dealer. I don't want them thinking that," I said sternly.

"After all this is over, ma'am, you can tell anyone who asks for the real truth. In the meantime, we need you to go along with us on this," he said in a calm but pleading tone.

"If I go along, what's going to happen next?"

"We're going to perp walk you out of here in handcuffs so we can

12

take you to the sheriff's office for further conversation."

"Are the handcuffs really necessary," I asked.

"Yes ma'am. It is protocol no matter who is being arrested," the sheriff said sheepishly.

"You will be destroying my reputation," I mumbled. "But I will go along with it if it gets the druggies out of here. This used to be a wonderful small town. I would like that to happen again."

"Yes ma'am."

I sat and watched the men search through my belongings, turning everything upside down and over. "If this is only for show, why are they tearing my place apart," I asked angrily.

"It has to look real," said Barry.

"Sheriff you need to see this," shouted a deputy who must have slipped into my bedroom without my noticing.

"You stay here, Ms. Spencer. I'll be right back," said Barry as he stood to leave the room.

I had no idea what was so important in my bedroom that required Barry's attention. I sat and waited for Barry to return.

"Ms. Spencer, why would you have these in your dresser drawer," asked the sheriff as he held up a couple bags of what looked like cocaine in front of me.

"What is that," I sputtered.

"Cocaine, and it is worth a lot of money," he explained.

"I don't do drugs. I don't buy drugs. I don't sell drugs. I have no idea where those came from unless your deputy put it there," I said in controlled tones as I tried to harness my temper.

"Have you had any company lately," the sheriff asked.

"No, I live alone but I think someone has been in here snooping. I noticed that some of my things had been moved out of place. Nothing was missing. The key that I have hidden in the fake rock in the flower bed was there. My nerves were a little frayed after that, but I just wrote it off as something I must have done and then forgot about it."

"When did that happen," asked the sheriff.

"A couple of days ago," I answered.

"Ms. Spencer, I know that the drugs are not yours. But, because they were found here during the search, I will have to arrest you for real," explained a sad Barry Hendricks, Chief of Police.

"Now, what am I supposed to do?" I answered as angry tears appeared in my eyes.

"I suggest you call a lawyer. In the meantime, we will check for prints on the plastic bags. Hopefully, that will give us an idea of who is doing this to you," said the sheriff.

"Who was the last person to visit you in your house," asked the chief.

"Let me think. Ginger and her family were here and that's about all. I don't have very many friends who just pop in on me," I said sadly.

"Well, I think you have been set up to take a bad fall. I will do everything I can to help you out of this mess, Louella," Barry said.

"Thanks, but you aren't going to keep me in jail, are you," I asked as fear raced down my spine.

"I have to, Ms. Spencer. I really don't have a choice. Now, if you will stand up, I will read you your rights and cuff you," said the solemn sheriff.

"Could you at least tell me which lawyer I should contact," I asked. My voice was breaking from the pressure on the lump in my throat. I was swallowing hard and often to keep that lump from bursting open and erupting into sobs.

Why would Ginger do this to me? I thought she was my friend. I thought to myself while the sheriff placed handcuffs on my wrists.

I was marched out in front of all the on-lookers who were my neighbors. The sheriff placed his hand on the top of my head, bending me forward, so I could fall into the police vehicle, which was what I had to do. I couldn't use my hands to keep my balance.

I'm an old lady. Did they think I was going to make a break for it?

I was so embarrassed. It was bad enough for them to ask me to pretend. But — when the pretend became real, I was beyond embarrassment. I kept my eyes to the ground. I didn't want anyone to see all of the shame that was filling my heart and soul.

As soon as the police vehicle arrived at the sheriff's office, I was taken to an interrogation room where I was pushed into a chair. My cuffs were removed from one wrist and I was attached to an apparatus protruding from the center of the table. It was very uncomfortable, but

I was sure that was their aim.

I sat in that room alone for what seemed to be a very long time. All I could do was look at the green-gray walls, and avoid looking at myself in the mirror that I knew had to be a two-way mirror. I wondered who was on the other side watching me.

Finally, Detective Mason entered the room.

"Ms. Spencer, I need you to tell me who you bought those drugs from," he said sternly.

"I didn't buy any drugs from anybody," I answered angrily.

"Then how do you explain the fact that the deputy found several bags of cocaine in your bedroom?" His tone was harsh.

"I don't know how they got there. I don't know who put them there. I do not and have never used any drugs that aren't prescribed by my doctor."

"If you didn't put them there, who did," demanded Detective Mason.

"Like I told the sheriff, the only visitors I have had in the last few days other than the deputy who found them are my neighbors, and they might have let themselves in when I was gone if they found my key," I answered almost in rote.

"Who are your neighbors," he snapped.

"Ginger Hampton and the three young people she calls her kids," I answered in monotone.

"Why do you say that she calls them her kids?"

"Because that's what the sheriff told me a couple of hours ago. I didn't know it until then," I answered sullenly.

"We need to know your dealer's name, Ms. Spencer. If you work with us, we will work with you," he said convincingly.

"What do you want me to do? I can't tell you the name of my dealer, because I don't have one. I would love to work with you, but I don't have anything to tell you except that those drugs aren't mine," I said loudly as I fought back the angry tears.

"Are you sure, Ms. Spencer? Are you sure you won't help us," he asked in a softer tone.

"I can't help you because I don't know anything! Now, I think I need a lawyer. You don't seem to understand that I have been set up. I

15

think I need a lawyer," I said in a forced, even tone.

"Who is you lawyer?"

"I need one assigned to me by the court," I said. "I don't have a lawyer on retainer. I didn't think I would ever need a criminal lawyer at my age of sixty-seven. Can you please let me go to the bathroom?"

"Yes ma'am. A deputy will escort you," he said in a defeated tone.

"Detective Mason?"

"Yes ma'am?"

"I really don't know where those drugs came from," I said solemnly.

"Yes ma'am," he grunted.

After the lady deputy led me to the washroom, I was taken to a holding cell where I was locked up with some fiercely, bedraggled females. Most of the ladies were high or drunk or both, and were not fit company for anyone.

My guess about the treatment that I was getting was that this was their way of getting me to talk. What they didn't seem to understand was that I would be happy to talk if I knew what to tell them. I moved to a corner of the cell and sat on the seat that was attached to the wall. My cellmates paid no attention to me, for which I was grateful.

I sat in that holding cell for a couple of hours as I waited for the next step to happen. It was so totally out of my control.

A flurry of activity caused me to rouse myself from my daydreaming about being at home in my little house on Valleyview Street. I looked to the front of the cell and saw Ginger Hampton and her so-called daughter being escorted to the adjoining cell.

Our gazes locked but no words were spoken.

A deputy appeared at the front of the cell I was in and he shouted my name.

"Louella Spencer, step forward."

"Yes, that's me," I shouted back at him.

When I reached the door, the deputy unlocked it, and I was allowed to exit without being handcuffed.

"What's going on," I asked.

"You are being released," said the deputy.

"Why?"

"The sheriff said so," he said.

The deputy took me to the same interrogation room I had been in earlier.

"The sheriff will be with you shortly," he said as he left the room.

I sat and stared at the mirror again, but this time, I wasn't attached to the table.

The door burst open and the sheriff entered.

"Louella, you are free to go," he said with a smile.

"Why?" I asked again.

"We caught your neighbors trying to remove their stash from their house. They thought we had locked up and departed from your house when your neighbors started moving their stock. We caught them red-handed," he said proudly.

"What about the drugs that you found in my house?" I asked. I needed to know how they got there.

"Ginger Hampton admitted to hiding them in your dresser one day when you were not home. It was her personal stash and she didn't want anyone to know about it. She said she knew it would be safe with you," he said.

"It's nice to know that the crooks trust me, too. Now — when can I go home?" I asked as I smiled.

"Right now. I'll drive you."

Second Chances

Victoria Fletcher

"Isn't there any way you can help me," Sandy asked as she tried to hold back the tears that were threatening to fall.

"I wish we could but we only have a limited amount of funds," said the lady at the Social Services office. "I will give you a list of some other places that you might be able to get help from."

Sandy Carver walked slowly back to her car as she read the list. She had already been to three of the five on the list. Those three were unable to help.

Sandy thought to herself, *I never dreamed my life would turn out like this – me on food stamps, living in my car, showering at the local Y. Not me. Not the girl voted most likely to succeed in high school.* Her mind drifted back to where it all began.

Sandy (Billings then) and Jeff Carver fell in love in their senior year of high school, and were married as soon as they graduated.

Jeff was not the husband he should have been. He verbally and mentally abused Sandy daily. He would tell her she needed to lose weight, do something with that mop of hair, fix up the house so he could have his friends over, and on and on.

"God, Sandy, you're a slob. Get it together, would you," Jeff said on more than one occasion.

"Jeff, I work all day. You could help me with the house and we

19

would both have a break," Sandy replied meekly.

"Housework is a woman's job. If you can't handle it, I guess I best be finding me someone who can," Jeff said.

This went on for five years.

Sandy went to talk with the pastor at the church she attended about getting marriage counseling. The pastor was more than happy to help. When Sandy went home and told Jeff she would like to try this, he refused. That was the first...and last time...that he hit her.

Sandy ended up in the ER that night. She called her pastor. He came to the hospital and told her he knew of a shelter where she could stay until she could get help to get away from Jeff. The pastor told her of abuse counseling sessions that were held at the church. She attended them regularly, and knew she needed to get a divorce from Jeff because he would never change. Well, at least if he wasn't willing to try, and he wouldn't.

Jeff came to the shelter to see her. He apologized over and over again and swore that he would never hit her again.

"I took your verbal and mental abuse for years because I was too ashamed to let people know what I was going through. I will not be hit. I grew up seeing that happen to my mom and told myself that would never happen to me, no matter what I had to do," Sandy said.

Sandy thought about the abuse her mom faced for years. Her step-dad would have started in on her if her mom hadn't protected her. Her mom told her to study hard and do well in school so she would be able to make something out of her life and not end up in circumstances like she had. That's when she really started focusing on her education and became the valedictorian of her high school class. Her thoughts came back to the present as Jeff was pleading with her.

"But it won't happen again," Jeff repeated.

"I know it won't because I'm not going back home with you. I am filing for divorce. If you don't want this to spread all over town, you will quietly give me my divorce," Sandy said.

When Sandy saw the look in Jeff's eyes, she closed and locked the door. He began pounding on the door and yelling, "Who do you think is going to want a used, ugly, fat woman that can't keep house or even give them any babies?"

Tears freely fell down Sandy's cheeks. How she had wanted a child. She had three miscarriages during their five years of marriage. Three little lives bound for heaven. Oh, how she longed to hold a little baby.

Sandy thought, *I can't bring a baby into this world I'm in. I have lost everything. I lost my husband (by choice). I lost my home and everything I owned (by Jeff's revenge). I am living in my car with clothes I picked up at a thrift store, where I worked to pay for them. I'm getting food from the local food bank. I lost my job after my divorce because I went through a time of depression. My boss said he couldn't keep me on with all my absences. That's what landed me at Social Services today.*

Unfortunately, Social Services wouldn't or couldn't help me. I'm not sure which.

Sandy went to the fourth place on the list that the Social Services lady gave her, and it was another food bank. She was thankful for their help, though. The sweet lady there helped her find things she didn't have to cook since she had nowhere to do that.

Next, she went to the last place on the list. It was called Second Chances. She thought it would be a thrift store, like the one where she had gotten clothes. When Sandy told the woman in charge about her circumstances, the woman said she could help.

"I will set you up with a room and temporary job," said Mrs. Corman. "The job could become permanent if you do it well and like it. The room is for four ladies that have to share one bathroom. You all must work out your schedule together. You will also receive three hot meals a day. If there are any problems, you will be asked to leave."

"That sounds wonderful, and there will be no problems," Sandy gushed. "I will work hard at my job, and I will help you here any way I can. Thank you so much for this opportunity."

After six months, Sandy was starting to enjoy her job and had worked her way up to a permanent position as secretary to the boss. He gave her a raise. She started saving every penny she could so she would be able to get back on her feet and out on her own once again.

Soon Sandy was able to rent a small apartment close to her job. She went back to Second Chances to pick up her things.

"I will miss you all so much," Sandy told Mrs. Corman and the ladies she had roomed with.

"You will be missed, but we are so glad things are working out for you," said Mrs. Corman.

"Yeah, this is what we all want to happen," said Judy, one of the ladies she shared the room with. "We all want to be able to be back on our own."

"You were a big part of making that happen for me," said Sandy. "I have been meaning to ask you who sponsors Second Chances. I would like to make a donation to support them in thanks for what you have done for me."

"It is one of the projects of Pastor Kirk from Morningside Baptist Church. Are you familiar with the church or the pastor," asked Mrs. Corman.

"Before I got divorced and hit the bottom, I attended that church and Pastor Kirk tried to help me. He was willing to have marriage counseling with Jeff and I but Jeff refused. That's when Jeff hit me. Pastor Kirk came to the hospital to pick me up and took me to a shelter. I wonder why he didn't bring me here," Sandy asked.

"I think he probably was going to, but I was full at the time," said Mrs. Corman.

"I think it is past time that I paid him a visit," Sandy said with a smile of pleasant surprise. After hugs and good wishes all around, Sandy left Second Chances to go to her new home.

Sandy went to church that Sunday and rededicated her life. She felt better than she had in years.

Everything seemed to be going well for Sandy. She was a hard worker and moved up in the company. She was now the assistant manager to the boss she had been secretary to. This came with another raise. During her time working there, she met a young man by the name of Billy Compton. They started attending church together and it wasn't long before they were a couple. They were married at the church on the most beautiful Saturday you could have asked for. Her life was definitely turning around.

Four years later, Sandy went to her ten-year high school reunion. When they were going through the superlatives and asked her if she felt as if 'Most Likely to Succeed' had fit her life, she proudly beamed, "It has, thanks to second chances."

Gumption

Lori C. Byington

On a chilly, early March around mid-morning in Bristol, Tennessee, early robins hop and twitter excitedly on the window sill outside a hospital window at Grayson Memorial Hospital. The last spring snow has begun to melt off the roof, and drops of water make a blop sound every two seconds. Myrtle Counts stirs drowsily and tries to rearrange herself in the stiff, uncomfortable hospital bed. *What is that smell piercing my nose? The stuff smells like plastic and alcohol going straight into my nostrils.* Still in a fog, she raises her right arm to swat the offensive smoke away from her face only to find she was hooked to an oxygen line like a Mallard on a Duck Dynasty hunting lanyard. Wincing, Myrtle tries to remove the bull ring from her nose, but the beastly device is stuck. Just the simple act of moving her arm is a chore. She is as sore as if she had been kicked in the chest by one of Tal's milk goats.

Suddenly, the door to Myrtle's hospital room swings open with a swoosh, and the clatter of plastic wheels heralds a tall nursing cart that looks more like a robot from *Lost in Space*. The device is followed by a short, rotund female.

"Well hello Mrs. Counts! How are you this morning," says a much too young nurse dressed in pink scrubs with brown teddy bears, and grinning from ear to ear. "I am Cindy Robinson and here to take care of you today. How do you feel?" she gushes a bit too enthusiastically.

23

Myrtle tries to blink her sky-blue eyes into focus and begins to tell her piece of mind, but her throat will not cooperate. She feels like she has swallowed coals from last week's church bar-b-que. Youngster Love quickly pours a cup of ice water into a styrofoam cup and holds it to Myrtle's lips.

"Take a small drink Mrs. Counts. You have had a tube down your throat for better than two hours, so you are probably tender there," Nurse Love says caringly.

Myrtle does as she is told. The cold water feels good going down her raw throat, and once she swallows, she begins to try to talk again. The coals have been doused, but her voice is still a bit hoarse. "What time is it," squeaks Myrtle. "Where is my husband, Tal?"

"Right here," comes a deep but tentative voice from behind happy Nurse Love. Tal's tired, gray-green eyes and rumpled clothes betray his smile. He looks as if he had either slept rolled up inside a haybale or not slept at all. Probably the latter, if Myrtle were to guess.

Nurse Love unceremoniously but deftly de-rings Myrtle's nose from the noxious oxygen line, and twists the tube out of sight. Myrtle takes a few deep breaths of air to clear the acrid smell from her nostrils. "Thanks," she whispers. "I was afraid I was going to up-chuck if I had to smell that plastic air any longer."

"I'll leave you two for a bit, but I have to bring your antibiotics and Tylenol in a few," notes Nurse Counts as she nods to Myrtle. With a whoosh she shoves the robot out of Myrtle's room and quietly closes the hospital room door.

Myrtle can see Tal's face and whispers, "I am fine but a tad bit sore."

Tal lets out a gust of air he has probably been holding for hours. "I am glad of it," he says and looks a little relieved. "Doc says all went as planned. Better than that ornery cow trying to birth that breeched calf a few months ago!" Tal grins.

His comparison makes Myrtle laugh. "Well," she says, "at least I don't have to nurse any young'un!" The mood lightens in the stark, chalky hospital room. Tal sits down on the rigid, green couch under the window and takes his wife's right hand. Myrtle sighs heavily and winces as she tries to turn toward her husband. "Ow! I need to remember to not put weight on my right side for a while," she says through gritted teeth.

Tal bends over to gently kiss Myrtle on her forehead. She smiles slightly and closes her blue eyes. "I am ready to get out of here," she whispers quite sternly.

Tal nods and coughs. "I am ready to take you home," he responds. He holds back tears of joy and relief, but a hard sniff gives away his emotions. Myrtle smiles and thinks, *I am ready to go home and get back to normal.*

* * *

The middle of May arrives with a force usually reserved for March's lion, but the chill does not bother Myrtle much because Tal has just pulled their '69 Packard into their driveway. Myrtle is finally home from the last blasted radiation treatment. Originally, she thought the required radiation treatments and the place down the road in Oak Ridge, Tennessee were going to be in cahoots, and she was not far off. As Myrtle excitedly begins to get out of the car, a gust of wind left over from February whooshes around from the back of the house and almost knocks her back into her seat.

Tal rushes to Myrtle's side, but she waves him off. "I am fine, thank you," she says tartly. Tal nods and grins at his wife's tenacity. Luckily, Myrtle's body is covered well with a navy and orange, University of Virginia ski toboggan on her bare, sparsely whiskered head and a newly crocheted shawl over her shoulders. She recalls when she finished her last treatment, not more than an hour ago, the nurse offered a shawl hand-made by women's circle meetings from the Episcopal church. Myrtle had chosen a blue-gray, brown with bits of dark pink mingled in the crocheting as her prize shawl. Grateful for the cover, she thinks, *If I have to go through that hell again to get a prize I will politely decline!*

Slowly, Tal helps her begin up the steps to the front porch. "Now honey," he warns, "let me help you." Myrtle snorts as if to say, 'I can do it on my own,' but she lets him take her arm. As they begin up the front steps to the porch of their home, Myrtle quickly notices, again, the front Williamsburg blue shutters still need to be painted along with the white porch stoop. *That job will have to wait until the weather gets warmer, I get stronger or a little of both.*

Daily radiation treatments have worn Myrtle plumb out, almost as much as the four chemotherapy treatments she endured every three weeks prior to beginning the radiation. She often said a quick "Thank you Jesus" because she did not have to have the "Red Devil" chemotherapy. Still, the Taxotere and Cytoxan had done a number on her blood cells, energy and, of course, her blond hair. The first time Myrtle realized her eye brows and eye lashes had gone AWOL with her hair, she was caught off guard. The peaked image staring back at her from the gilded-framed mirror was a complete stranger.

The long drive in the '69 Packard to Wake Forest Baptist Hospital had become almost routine during her four-hour chemotherapy sessions, and Myrtle and Tal always joked that the nurses and doctors at Wake Forest would *not* appreciate her University of Virginia toboggan. Still, Myrtle would not miss the trips from Goodson up Interstate 81 through Wytheville, Virginia and on into Winston Salem, North Carolina. She knew Tal would not miss the monotony of the drive either, even though the landscapes along the interstates were beautiful in April and early May. For miles and miles, the Bradford pear trees, jonquils, tulips, spring onions, and dogwoods seemed to dance together while they combined colors of pinks, whites, yellows, and every shade of green in a box of Crayola Crayons. Now, though, Myrtle is ready to get on with life again — with or without hair!

* * *

On a warm, late-August afternoon, Tal is contentedly painting Sherwin Williams Westhighland White on the railing on the front stoop of his and Myrtle's house. They have shared and made this place home for nigh on 31 years. The painting was long overdue, but Myrtle's breast cancer diagnosis back in the fall had derailed any plans they had back then. Chemotherapy and radiation treatments were finished in late spring, and all Myrtle needs to do is take a pill every day to ward off unwelcome, sneaky hormones. Tal smiles to himself and thinks, *I am sure glad Myrtle has gumption and grit. She had a plan and, by gosh, she did more than walk through fire. She ran all the way to the end.*

Tal's peaceful monotony of painting is suddenly interrupted. "Tal! Come help me with this basket of apples please!" screams Myrtle, who is obviously panicked. Tal looks up from painting the front stoop to the area where he hears his wife's voice, but he cannot directly see her.

"Tal!!" yells Myrtle again, this time with urgency. Tal throws down his paint brush, which splatters the green grass with a nice white wash, and runs toward Myrtle's voice. All of a sudden, Tal hears a whoomph and a high-pitched shriek. Fearing the worst, he runs to the small apple orchard, where he imagines he will find Myrtle. When he gets to the area he does find his wife she is hanging upside down with arms and legs wrapped around a tree branch about five cubits above the ground. Her blond hair is beginning to grow back, so her small curls bounce as she grunts heavily and attempts to hold on to the tree limb.

Tal begins to laugh hysterically and snorts out, "What in the world happened?"

Myrtle hisses, "This is not funny! I was trying to reach the top limbs to fill the bushel basket with the ripe Macintoshes and I tipped over the ladder!" Tal looks at the broken basket and a cascade of red and green orbs are blanketing the ground under Myrtle. Tal then sees the ladder has fallen so hard on its right side one of the legs became cock-eyed and splintered. The ladder leg will need major woodworking to right it.

"Maybe I will just shoot the ladder and put it out of its misery," Tal says aloud with a laugh.

"Well, don't just stand there a-gaping! Help me down before I fall on my backside," Myrtle yells with another grunt as she tries to tighten her short legs around an uncooperative apple tree limb. Chuckling under his breath, Tal reaches up to assist his bride. He is just tall enough to put his hands along Myrtle's back and bum to offer support.

"Now let go of your left arm from the branch," Tal instructs, still laughing, "and wrap your arm 'round my neck." With another grunt, Myrtle does as she is told. She does not look Tal's way, though, and promptly smacks him on the nose with her left hand. "Ouch," yells Tal. The pain causes him to drop his right arm a bit, which causes Myrtle's back to be fair game for the ground below.

27

Without the help of her left arm, her right arm slips down the side of the rough tree limb. Hanging only by her short legs, Myrtle again screeches like an owl, "Tal!" Tal looks up to see Myrtle swinging wildly from the branch with a look of wide-eyed panic on her face. Quickly, Tal reaches for Myrtle again and catches her waist just as her legs give way from the tree. Since they were both off kilter, Tal and Myrtle klutzily crash onto the ground and onto the array of spilled Macintoshes. "Ow," they cry in unison.

Myrtle's blue eyes show hints of laughter as she looks down at her handsome husband who is awkwardly smashed beneath her. "Well, thanks for being my knight in shining armor, Sir Talmadge!" Myrtle laughs.

Tal grunts and rolls out from under his wife. "You are most welcome Lady Myrtle, Princess of the Pommes! Anytime you need," Tal says and grins so big his smile could out-flash all the lightnin' bugs flittin' around on a hot summer's night. The pair look at each other, but their smiles slowly fade at bit.

Myrtle breaks eye contact, "Finally, we can laugh and do things together again. I feel well, and feel stronger every day."

Tal looks lovingly at his bride, "I always knew you would beat any nasty ailing that came your way. Now, what're we goin' to do about that poor ladder?"

28

Just Drive

Linda Hudson Hoagland

I counted the cash I'd taken from the ATM and turned around. My next-door neighbor was standing before me with a gun in his hand.

"Mack, what are you doing," I whispered to him.

"Getting some spending money, and you happen to be the source today," he growled.

"You could have borrowed money from me, you know that," I said in an even softer voice.

"Yeah I know that, but then I would have to pay you back," he said angrily.

"Please don't do this," I pleaded.

"Just give me the money," he snarled.

"Then what?"

"Then — I'll have to kill you," he answered.

I wanted to run, but he was standing too close to me. I backed up a bit and he stepped forward. My knees were getting weak and I hoped I wasn't going to fall to the ground. I was afraid the sudden movement would cause him to fire his gun point blank at me.

"Mack, just take the money and pay me back if and when you can," I whispered.

I glanced around and there was no one approaching the ATM. Ordinarily there would be people trying to withdraw money from the

29

machine but not this time.

"Get in your car, Lynn. I'll be right behind you," he said as he pushed the gun toward me.

"You don't need to do this," I said when I reached my car.

"Unlock the door," he whispered harshly with spittle flying through the air.

I didn't have electronic door locks, so after I unlocked the driver's side door, I opened it and reached inside to unlock the rear door.

"Okay, where do you want me to take you," I asked weakly.

"Just drive. I'll tell you when to stop," he said in a less angry sounding tone.

I started the engine, shifted the gear to drive, and eased out of the parking lot.

My mind was racing from one probability to another, with all of the endings being death.

"Watch your speed," Mack said as he watched the speedometer from the seat behind me.

I glanced down and saw that I wasn't driving too fast.

He must think I'm driving too slowly.

I pushed the gas pedal a little more to pick up the pace. I needed to get the attention of the police but with him watching my speedometer, that wasn't going to happen.

I slid my hand down to the button that would activate the emergency flashers.

"What are you doing," Mack snapped.

"I'm going to rub my knee. It's hurting. I must be sitting in a strain," I said as I winced from a make-believe, sharp, shooting pain.

"Keep your hands on the steering wheel," he snarled.

"Okay," I said as I raised my lowered hand, pushing the button to start the flashers as I did so.

People started watching my car as it passed because of the flashing lights.

"What did you do?"

"Nothing. I put my hand up on the steering wheel like you told me to," I said excitedly.

"You did something," he said as he caught sight of the flashing signal on the dashboard inside the car.

He pushed the gun forward from between the two front bucket seats.

"Turn them off now," he hissed.

"What are you talking about?" I asked feigning surprise at the accusation.

"The emergency lights, turn them off now, Lynn," he said angrily with spittle flying from his mouth.

"Where? How do I do that?" I was continuing to pretend to not know what he was talking about.

"Put your hand back down where you had it before and find the button. Don't act so stupid. You know where it is. Do it NOW."

"All right, all right. Why don't you let me pull the car over, get out, and you can go on your way? I won't even call the cops, Mack. Please let me out of the car," I said in a calming tone. I was trying to temper his anger.

"You know I can't do that. Make a left turn here," he snarled.

My heart sank. He was heading me toward the mountains and Hungry Mother State Park.

He scooted up on his seat, lifting his rear end up to position himself to look over my shoulder at the gas gauge.

"Good, full tank," he whispered in my ear.

"Yes, it is," I added.

"Keep driving till we get to the park, then we're going for a long walk," he said with a little less anger.

I had no idea how I was going to get out of this mess.

I had known Mack for a few years as a reclusive neighbor who kept to himself, meaning that we never got beyond the 'hi – how are you?' stage. I really liked him living next door because I always felt safe for some strange reason. Now, I was trying to figure out how I could have been so wrong.

"Why do you need the money, Mack? Why would you need to steal it," I asked.

"Shut up," he snapped.

That's just what I did. I drove around the hairpin curves, up and over the three mountains until we arrived at Hungry Mother State Park.

31

When I drove up to the ranger booth for admittance, I paid the nominal fee for entrance to the rest of the park. I thought I knew where he would make me park the car, and then we would be on foot to who knows where.

"Keep driving till I tell you to stop," he said sternly.

"Don't you want me to pull into one of the parking lots," I asked hopefully.

"No — just drive!" He was getting angry again.

I drove.

At the top of the mountain I saw a pull over spot built so sight seers could look out across the beautiful mountains and valleys. Normally the magnificent view would make me happy to be able to scan the sight. But it wasn't so beautiful today. Actually, it was scary. No — it was downright terrifying.

Was he going to push me off the top?

He didn't tell me to pull over so I drove past that possibility.

About half way down the backside of the mountain, he told me to pull over onto a space that was barely big enough to park the car.

"Get out," he said as he prodded me with the gun.

"Here?"

"Get out now," he shouted into my ear.

"Okay," I shouted back at him, except this time I was the one getting angry.

"There's a path over there," he said as he waved his gun to point out the way to go.

My knees were beginning to weaken again, and I wasn't sure if I was going to be able to walk the weed covered path.

When the barrel of the gun punched into my back, I moved.

We followed the path with me praying that it wouldn't come to an end because I knew that meant death for me. I wobbled along the path on severely weakened knees. It took all of my concentrated effort to propel my body along the path that would lead me to my tragic demise.

"Mack," I whispered.

"What," he snapped

"Can't we stop and talk about this," I pleaded.

"No — keep moving," he said in a raspy voice.

32

I took a deep breath and plodded on as I silently prayed for help.

We were moving deeper and deeper into the forest, and the underbrush was grabbing at my skin, scratching me so badly that blood was oozing from the many briar-caused cuts. A steady stream of tears was rolling down both of my cheeks. I was afraid to keep moving but I knew I couldn't stop.

I glanced behind me and noticed that he was not as close to me as he had been.

The light was starting to fade. I glanced at my wrist watch and discovered it was late afternoon.

"Time flies when you're having fun," I mumbled.

Maybe I can go over behind the bushes to answer the call of nature and then just run.

"I'm going to go over here to relieve myself," I shouted to my kidnapper.

"Okay, but hurry up," he said angrily.

I noisily made my way to an area where there would be some privacy; I did not stop and squat. Instead, I made my way with all the stealth I could muster to what I hoped would be freedom.

I could feel the darkness drawing me into its pouch. Soon the string would be drawn at the top of my wooded world and it would be totally dark because I could see no sign of the moon and twinkling stars. It had become cloudy, and the clouds smothered what little light that was left.

When I tripped over a vine stretched across my walking space, I decided I needed to stop. Going further could be very dangerous. I found a tree where I could crawl under the thick brush and settle my back against the trunk to rest, hide, and wait for help.

No one knew I was in Hungry Mother State Park, hiding from a nut with a gun.

Who in the world would look for me in this place?

The brush was rustling; twigs were snapping; someone was coming.

I willed myself to be smaller. I needed to vanish. I ducked my head down, pulled my legs in, and prayed it wasn't Mack.

Whoever was thrashing through the brush wasn't trying to be quiet. My heart told me that Mack would be moving as quietly as he could, so he could sneak up on me. I raised my head up to look for a hint of color that might represent a shirted person hiking for fun and exercise. *I'm getting too old for this foolishness*, I thought as I continued to search for the noise maker. The bushes parted in front of me and a park ranger stood before me with his hands on his hips.

My mouth dropped open as I whispered, "Please help me."

"Are you Lynn?" asked the park ranger.

"Yes, are you looking for me, I hope?"

"Yes ma'am. Mack told us you were probably lost out here," the park ranger explained.

"He did. Did he tell you anything else," I asked as a tinge of fury flooded my body.

"He said you gave him a ride, and that you were scared away by a strange man who was trying to rob you," he explained further.

"Yes, yes. He was right about that. Where is Mack?"

"He said he would wait at the ranger station for you to return. He needed a ride back to his home, if it is okay with you," said the park ranger.

"Did he tell you anything else about the man who frightened me," I asked as I started walking down the path, led by the park ranger.

"He said he didn't get a real good look, but you would be able to describe him," answered the park ranger.

"Yes, I am. I'll do that when we get back there. I do need to pick up my car on the way."

"No ma'am, we need to go to the ranger station first, and then I will take you to your car," he explained slowly.

"That's fine," I said.

He didn't ask me any more questions while we were finding our way back to a gravel road where his vehicle was located. We climbed into the vehicle and he drove me to the ranger station. When I walked in, I was surprised that Mack was still waiting there.

"Hey, Lynn," said Mack. "Are you okay?"

"Yes," I said. All I could come up with was the one word answer. I didn't know what else to expect from Mack.

"Now that we are all here, could you tell me what happened," said the park ranger.

I looked at Mack. He lowered his head and avoided eye contact with me.

"Let Mack start out with the explanation," I said softly.

"No, Lynn needs to tell you what happened," Mack stammered.

"I won't unless you start it out. You asked me for a ride. Remember, Mack?"

"Yeah, okay, Lynn gave me a ride to the park. When we got here that's when everything else happened. You need to tell him the next part," said Mack.

I looked at Mack and could tell he was worried about what I was going to tell the park ranger. "The man was a vagrant and he was so dirty, I really couldn't tell you what he looked like. His hair was filthy and so matted that I couldn't tell you anything about the color. He was so hunched over that I couldn't tell how tall he was. His clothes were raggedy and hanging off all around him. I know it's not much help, but that's all I can tell you," I said as I glanced at the park ranger searching his face to see if he believed me.

"Did you see his eye color?" asked the park ranger.

"No, I can't say that I did. He scared me so much by poking what appeared to be a gun at me."

"Did you see a gun?" asked the park ranger.

"No sir. I saw what I thought was a gun," I answered.

"I'll keep this info on hand," said the park ranger.

"Is it all right if I go get my car so I can take Mack home?"

"Yes ma'am. We will keep an eye out for the vagrant, but I can almost guarantee that he has moved on," said the park ranger.

The three of us climbed into the park ranger's vehicle so he could drive us back to my car.

Once Mack and I were situated in my car, I waited for an explanation. The silence between us was like a wall.

Finally, he removed a brick from the wall by saying, "Thanks, Lynn." That was followed by the crumbling of the walled structure.

"You are welcome. Now, tell me why all of this happened," I said sternly.

"I needed money," Mack said.

"I know that. What was the money for?"

"Rent," he answered.

"Is that all? You know I would be happy to loan you rent money," I said harshly.

"I needed to pay all the utilities, too," he explained.

"You have a job, don't you," I probed.

"No, I was laid off and I haven't found another one yet. The landlord is going to evict me, and then I won't have a place to live," he said sadly.

"Let's put our heads together, Mack, and we will find you some help. In the meantime, I will loan you what you need to pay right away," I said with sincerity.

"I won't be able to pay you back for a while," he whispered in a voice that was cracking with emotion.

"You do handy work for other people, don't you?"

"Yes, but that has slowed down to a trickle."

"Good, that means you can do some odd jobs for me. You can work off your debt that way."

"You're not going to turn me in to the police for kidnapping you at gunpoint?"

"No, that wasn't you. That was some old, dirty guy I can't identify, remember?"

Bess's Story

Julia Parsell

There it is. I can't believe I found it after all these years. She was standing tall, slim, and graceful in the dappled light. As I walked over, I remembered the story my grandmother told me when she first encountered her, and that story will never leave my mind.

Two years earlier

It seemed like an ordinary day, the birds beckoned me outside, and I pulled a strand of hair from my mouth. It was March and the wind was biting. I took a few minutes to gaze at the sky, follow the chirps, and see a chickadee hopping from branch to branch. Gratitude, yes, that's what I felt even though it wasn't like my life looked very hopeful. Sure, I had quit cigarettes, mind you for the cost savings rather than the health benefit, and yes that was something to be grateful about. My fingernails had grown and were no longer nubs. I had some food in the fridge and pantry, and I always said that made me feel like a rich woman. My car was old, but it ran. My clothes were not new, but they fit. Yes, I had a lot to feel grateful about.

Four years earlier

Yes, I wanted this. Yes, I orchestrated it, but wow did it hurt. My life in the city had proven to be glamorous and I loved all the choices of food, clothing, and the ever stream of energy from Broadway to the lower east side, to my solitude walking in the numerous parks. I was living the dream, my career provided a nice apartment and I appreciated looking over the river, seeing the twinkle of man-made lights and even the honking horns. My closet held so much it sometimes overwhelmed me. Wasn't this what my education prepared me for—a sense of financial freedom, choices, and long-range views? It is interesting how being numb can hurt.

I fluffed my pillow, looked at my stubby nails, and then glanced over to the empty pack of cigarettes. Where did they even come from and why? I don't want to smoke; I don't want to bite my nails – something just doesn't feel right. I am lonely, yes, but that's not the end of the world. Had I dreamed of grandmother last night? It felt like she was right here with me.

The coffee smell wafted down the street as I neared my usual spot on the corner. Life's simple pleasure awaited me.

"Good morning Bess," the barista smiled as I walked through the door. A line was already at the counter, but it never failed that one of the gals behind the counter would welcome me as I entered.

"Your usual," she asked, as I was up next to order.

"Yes, thanks Allie!"

"You look very smart today," Allie winked, "big presentation?"

"You're so observant, Allie. Yes, my design is being considered for the new wing of the museum, and I will offer some more details this morning. I'm both excited and very nervous. I'd rather stay in my office and dream about it than talk about it."

"Bess, I love your work and I'm always in awe of how you can create such interesting spaces in obscure and forgotten corridors."

"Thanks, Allie. You always cheer me, and thanks for the fantastic latte!"

"Best of luck today, Bess!"

Wow, I thought as I walked out of the coffee shop. Allie is so uplifting to me, and from her perspective my life is pretty sweet. What was missing? Why couldn't I shake this numbness?

I needed a cigarette. *Ugh, here I go again. No,* I screamed inside, *this is not me. This is not me.*

I woke suddenly. My grandmother again? This is the second time this month. I needed to call her, something must be up. I knew the last time I talked with Mom, grandmother was still spry and tending her garden. The dream was so vivid; grandmother was telling me something. I could see her home, her little garden, the screened in back porch with the big quilt on the cushy chair, but I couldn't remember anything she was saying as we walked in the woods. This was so strange.

When I stopped by and got my latte, Allie was not there that morning. I missed her; she was such a bright light for me. I walked into the office and noticed there was an unusual stir. Was Becky crying? Oh, my, something's not right. Jane opened her door, greeted me, and asked me to come in.

"Bess, this isn't going to be easy, so prepare yourself. I hoped to have had this matter settled, but it didn't go as I had expected. I'm closing the firm and moving back to San Antonio. I know you knew this was a possibility, and I'm sorry that it is so sudden. But, this is something I must do. You are a talented woman with great potential, I'll give you a very good reference."

Possibility, I thought to myself. Probability, no, I hadn't let my mind go there. So, I sat there stunned, thinking *I don't feel numb in this moment. I need a cigarette.*

So just like that, my life in the city changed. I looked out the window of my high rise and breathed deeply. After the third dream about grandmother, I decided it was the right time to fly home to the mountains and visit her. I could visualize those blue ridges, see the red buds, and remember the daffodils that surrounded the posts near her driveway. Yes, I was going home.

Synchronicities, not just happenstance, but also God's appointments for us — how is it that most often we don't recognize them until we look back and then say, 'that must have happened for a reason'? The dreams of grandmother, the office closing, my numbness, the cigarettes that I really despised, all of these worked together as a message for my life.

Eventually I realized why the numbness existed — I had failed to forgive a wrong. Because I hadn't forgiven, the pain had eventually developed into numbness. Numbness is not friendly. Some may think that if you are devoid of feeling that is a good thing, but no, it is equally painful. It's a deep step down from grief and loss. I knew I needed to feel again, but couldn't find my way, so biting my nails and smoking eased that need and thus facilitated the numbness.

Visiting with grandmother allowed me the best education ever. She may have talked in this manner before, but I didn't have ears to listen. I remembered as a young child looking at her and thinking she was a bit quirky, but oh, how I always loved her. In my older age, her words resonated and gave me hope.

"Elizabeth," grandmother never picked up the nickname I carried with me since childhood, "I'm so pleased you got my message."

"Grandmother, how did you send your message? I can't remember what you said."

"Oh, Elizabeth, you know. It was in your dreams. I prayed for you, visualized you well and happy, and trusted that you would recognize it was time for us to talk."

"Grandmother, have you always had this 'power'? I'm curious as to how you developed it, and how you're always content with your life."

"Well sweetie, it's time to learn. Elizabeth, I'm happy to have you here and hope you'll spend some time with me in the woods periodically. Let's make it a date. We will come together at regular times that allow you to also work, rest, and play some too."

Grandmother graciously offered me a room in her cottage with some prerequisites.

I smiled and offered her a huge thankful hug.

I quickly found a serving position in a local farm to table restaurant. My days of waiting tables during college were paying off. It was such a funny thing to think what paid my bills during higher education, was now offering me a living for a new education. I guess life is cyclical in many ways, like the frond as it opens from the earth after a long winter's sleep.

The first day in the woods, grandmother and I just walked, smelled

40

some flowers, grasped rosemary as we walked past it, and let its fragrance waken our mind and heart. I remembered a bit of this when I used to visit grandmother in my youth.

"Elizabeth, everything is teeming with life, even the rocks. When we take time to walk in nature, it can speak to us, teach us, and refresh us. We just need to be willing to listen, and that takes being still. It's a practice with huge benefits. It may seem like you're doing nothing, but in fact everything is being accomplished as it should be within you."

It's so interesting that Grandmother never asked me why I smoked, and when I told her I often felt numb, she never inquired why. I've been so used to so many questions about my life from friends and other family members, it was refreshing to 'just be' in her presence.

Back in the cottage, I noticed a framed piece of art on her mantle. The colors were vivid and the calligraphy subtle, "Trauma is not actually what happens, but the way it is remembered." I wondered what story this has to tell for grandmother. I never really thought of grandmother as a person working through any type of trauma, she was my grandmother and that is how I thought of her. I imagine that is possibly why she was so gracious and didn't prod me. It was always comforting to be in her presence. I hoped maybe one day I would learn more about the artwork.

"It's called practicing presence. I've had many teachers in my life, and there are some common threads in them all. I've learned from those that walked these paths before us, the natives of this land. Also, many wise voices from the East beckoned me to listen, their voices taught as Jesus Christ taught. Many of us know those teachings in these beautiful Appalachian Mountains. Real truth is not just for a few to hold and share with the masses. Real truth is revealed in each individual's heart. It cleanses, purifies, and when present in your life, transforms. Elizabeth, you can trust my words, but you must practice presence in order to make it real for yourself."

I stooped down and began stroking a plant as I processed what Grandmother was saying.

"It is interesting that you are drawn down to this common plant right under your foot. Are you familiar with all it has to offer you, more than just the beauty of green on your path?"

"Not really,' I smiled, thinking she should really know this, because grandmother had often pointed out certain plants throughout her lifetime.

"This is plantain and a true friend to anyone walking in the woods or spending a lot of time in nature. A poultice of this will take the sting of a bee right away or soothe a mosquito bite."

One year after being with grandmother, my life was feeling fresh. I patted the car that I purchased from generous tips saved from the restaurant. She had some age, quite a bit actually, but I liked her character. It is so strange to think about how I spent every dime I received in the city on all the stuff I thought I needed. Now, the simple things brought me pleasure and my wants no longer drove me.

I remembered that one day grandmother and I had a talk that helped my life change from numb to this new feeling of fresh.

"Grandmother, thank you again for all you have taught me in the past six months and for a comfy room. I feel that I have some clarity now."

"Elizabeth, I'm here to listen whenever you are ready to share." Grandmother looked up from arranging the wildflowers in the large, clear Mason jar, and tenderness oozed from her heart straight through her eyes into mine.

Tears welled up in my eyes dropping onto the local women's magazine I was reading. "I haven't been able to put it into words until now, Grandmother. I'm still unsure that I can, but I feel I have to."

"Don't rush it, hurt takes time to work its way out and your tears are part of the cleansing process. When you're ready, just speak what feels right, and if it needs to come out fast and furious that's ok too."

Fast and furious it did. It was a regurgitation and I can barely remember what I did say. It was time, and I was ready. A safe space allowed me to not be fearful that my hurts would be held against me or rise up and slap me in the face. Grandmother assured me that healing was a process of becoming whole. When emotions are buried they steal parts of our self, and we become disoriented not sure what we feel any more.

"Here Elizabeth, take these things with you and have a nice long bath. When you release so much emotion, it's very beneficial to clear the energy around your body."

42

She handed me baking soda, sea salt, and sage essential oil. The glowing candles and soft music welcomed me as I drew my warm bath. My body relaxed and my emotions eased.

Months later, Becky allowed me to design a "couples" room in her farm to table restaurant. I took one of her rooms and created a private space for three separate tables. With a couple of whimsical partitions of color and design, along with large swaths of fabric, each table was its own oasis. Candles, a small fountain of water flowing over rocks with moss, and a cleverly disguised speaker for relaxing instrumental sounds offered the couples privacy and comfort on the cushioned chairs. We had a number of well-known folks that frequented the restaurant, as well as couples that some in our mountain community considered risqué. So, this room held a sense of mystery. Its own outside entrance meant that one never knew just whom might be dining. As a result of this lush space, my services were requested in numerous other places, some local and some not. Thus my savings grew and my time with my grandmother was coming to a close. I had spotted my own plot of land with a cottage at the bottom of the hill where I could continue my walks in the woods, grow a garden, and just be.

I had another idea that I passed on to grandmother. My time with her was foundational to my healing, as she loved me unconditionally and showed me how to live close to the land. As a result, my satisfaction with just living and not accumulating emerged as my everyday experience. One might say it was balanced and peaceful.

"Grandmother, have you ever considered renting your room out to others who might benefit from your love and wisdom? Your connection to the Earth, the healing tonics you taught me, how to overcome the cigarette habit, are just some of the life changing experiences I have had with you. There is a young woman at the restaurant that could benefit from your nurturing."

Grandmother did indeed offer her room up to Kacey, and the transformation that occurred was remarkable. Kacey moved on and Cindy moved in, and thus it continued for these past four years.

Then that one day came as I was walking on the hill behind my cottage that I spotted her. She was just as grandmother had told me. Solitary, still, graceful, and very pink.

"One day you will find a treasure in the woods, Elizabeth, and it will be a symbol for you. You will know it when you see it, and it will call to you deep within your heart. It will represent all that life has to hold for you and your purpose for living will be known."

Until I spotted this slender beauty, I had forgotten Grandmother even telling me those words years ago. Now, as I sat down beside her I realized that she had planted a thought in my mind that was like a seed, it needed to be nurtured, and grow, and then be realized. My purpose was to be at peace within myself, to stop striving, and to allow.

As I practiced this, my life would unfold in spontaneous and fluid ways.

Pretty Ribbons

Cheryl Livingston

Part 1 – Stella

What a good day this will be, I thought to myself. Instead of my usual chores of caring for my younger sisters and brother, I had been assigned the task of going to Miz Vertie's house to pick up a hair ribbon she had borrowed from my mother. She was going to be married soon and she wanted to look nice when she met her future in-laws. My mother, Rosa, had several beautiful ribbons that her suitors had given to her before she married my paw. *Mommy must have been so beautiful then*, I thought wistfully as I fingered my plain, brown hair. My reverie was broken as Miz Vertie offered me a glass of cool water and a small cookie. Beaming with pleasure, I took the cookie and nibbled slowly, trying to make the treat last.

Tucking the ribbon in my apron pocket, I said good-bye and headed home. My path took me directly in front of the Cranberry Iron Mine, which worked the largest deposit of ore in the south. Although the area was noisy and dusty, I dawdled as I walked past. It was so different from my usual days of farming and housework, that I didn't want to miss a moment of the humming activity. My paw always told me I was "a nosy little thing," and I guess he was right, because I sure liked to see

45

and hear all that I could. With my eyes glued to the bustle of the mine, it's amazing that I even noticed the item at my feet.

"Mommy will love this," I said to myself as I picked up a silvery tube from the gravel road. Skipping home with my treasure, I could just imagine how lovely it would look hanging from a chain around my mother's neck. Our village, nestled in the Appalachian Mountains of western North Carolina, was depressed even before the depression years, so pretty things were few and far between.

My eight-year old heart swelled with pride as mommy accepted my shiny gift with delight. "Thank you, Stella," she said softly. Smiles from her, like the pretty things that I loved, were rare and treasured.

Wanting to help, my sister Annie found the hammer, and my youngest sister Mae carried the small nail that mommy would use to pierce the cylinder. We all gathered around her as she worked, not suspecting that this one act would shatter our worlds. For what we did not know, in our young and uneducated minds, is that what I had found was a blasting cap. Used by the Cranberry Iron Mine, blasting caps triggered the dynamite that sent tons of dirt and rocks flying into the air.

With the first blow of the hammer, the blasting cap ignited, causing an explosion that knocked us all to the floor with an ear ringing, head spinning explosion! With wobbly legs, my sisters and I got to our feet, but my mommy did not. As I gazed around the room with unfocused eyes, the sound of screaming gradually became louder than the ringing in my ears, and I finally understood that my beautiful mommy was lying in a pool of blood, and — where was her hand?

Oh God, where was her hand? WHERE WAS HER HAND?

I looked over at my sisters, both in shock, and saw that their dazed little faces were covered in blood and matter. I fell back to my knees over my mommy's body and tore off my apron to use as a make-shift bandage for the stump at her wrist. Oh God, the screaming wouldn't stop...if only the screaming would stop, I could think of what to do. I was eight — I had bandaged my sisters' bumps and scrapes before, but what was I supposed to do about this? My own screams finally reached my consciousness as I was able to cry out, "Mommy! Mommy! WAKE UP MOMMY!" I clutched her wrist with all my strength as my screams became sobs.

Our neighbor, Mr. Frye, alerted by my screams, had to physically pry my hands from my mother's arm as he picked me up out of the floor. Mrs. Frye, with a pale, somber face, hustled me and my sisters away from our house and into her own kitchen. I sat dazedly at her table as she cleaned up my sisters and put them to bed.

As I waited, I looked down at my own blood covered hands...my two hands...I still had two hands...but now mommy only had one hand... and it's my fault! I began to rock back and forth with a low moan, "Oh God, it's all my fault! If I hadn't picked up that shiny tube, mommy would still have her hand!"

Mrs. Frye, who had finished ministering to my sisters, knelt in front of me, and began talking in a low, calming voice. She told me that my mother would be okay and that it was not my fault. Over and over, she said those words, until finally my rocking ceased and my body slumped with exhaustion. Sweet Mrs. Frye then took off my bloody clothes and washed my face and body. Wrapping me in a blanket, she held me in her arms as she rocked me to sleep in the wooden rocker on her front porch.

We continued to stay with the Fryes for several days. My sisters and I were still in shock, and no matter how silly Mr. Frye acted, I would not, could not, laugh. Mrs. Frye tempted us with many sweet treats, but I would not, could not, smile. How could I smile when I was responsible for this terrible thing that had happened to my mother? Everyone was going to hate me for what I had done. I hated myself for what I had done. Every night I prayed a hundred times for my hand to be gone instead of hers, but every morning my hand was still there.

As I was returning from gathering eggs for Mrs. Frye one morning, I saw my Paw standing on the porch. Eggs and apron flying, I ran to him, ready to leap into his arms, but the sadness in his eyes stopped me cold.

"Paw," I asked quaveringly. To my relief, he hunkered down and held out his arms for me. Wrapped in his bear hug, I felt like I could finally breathe again. Maybe he didn't hate me. I pulled back slightly and asked, "Mommy?" To my frustration, all he said was, "Get your sisters and let's go home." I desperately wanted to see Mommy, but what if she wouldn't forgive me? What if she hated me? With those thoughts

47

coursing through my mind, the walk from the Frye's home to our own seemed both too long and too short all at the same time.

Paw pushed open the screen door and I saw Mommy sitting in her rocker, quiet and still. My little heart couldn't take any more suspense. With tears falling down my cheeks, I fell at her feet, crying. "I'm sorry, Mommy. I'm so sorry. Please forgive me." My little sisters, seeing my tears, began crying too. "I'll help you even more now, Mommy. I'll learn to cook, and I'll get the girls ready in the morning, and I'll get the eggs, and I'll do the milking and...." My voice trailed off as I could sense this was not what Mommy needed to hear right now. I quieted both my sisters, as well as myself, and continued to sit at her feet with my head bowed. The haunting nightmares of the past week were replaying behind my eyes, so I screwed up my courage and took a quick glimpse upward. Her wrist was wrapped in a neat, clean bandage and it didn't look nearly as bad as the picture my nightmares had painted. Catching my breath and releasing it in a sigh, I quickly looked down again, her silence ringing in the room. Just as I thought I couldn't bear it another moment, she moved her remaining hand and placed in on my head. I looked up at her face this time, seeing sad and mournful eyes – but there was also something else there.

The horror that had locked my heart into a vise began to loosen as I looked into those eyes. I could hardly dare to believe it – yes great pain was there, but in the beautiful face of my mother I was overcome with the compassion, love, and forgiveness I saw there.

I began to cry.

Part 2 – Rosa

What a good day this will be, I thought to myself. Stella was away from the house on an errand and the other kids were playing in the creek. That meant I had a few precious moments to myself. I pulled out my mirror and set it on the kitchen table. Pinching my cheeks and examining my face with a critical eye, I decided that even at twenty-four, I was still a beautiful woman. After releasing my hair from its serviceable bun, I sat in front of the mirror, my brush and collection of pretty ribbons temporarily forgotten as I began to reminisce.

All the boys wanted to be my beau, and they knew the way to my heart was through the colorful ribbons I loved to wear in my dark, curly hair. At the Grange Hall dances, my card would be filled in the first few minutes — and oh, how I loved to dance! There was no feeling in the world like spinning across the dance floor, skirts and hair ribbons flying.

I could have had a different beau every week, but I wasn't ready to settle down — at least, not until Dane came to town. He was tall and handsome and strutted about like a rooster. All the girls wanted him, but I was the one that played hard-to-get, flipping my hair and pretending to ignore his charms. Deep inside though, I knew I wanted him too. Just catching his glance during class would make me go breathless. Gradually I dropped my guard, and soon he was walking me home from school. I had been kissed before — *many times*, I thought with a smile, but his kiss was different. I was head over heels in love and already planning our life together, so it seemed natural when our relationship moved to the next step. For several months I was gloriously happy, until I realized that I had a problem.

As Dane walked me home the next day, he stopped, circled my waist and whirled me around, knowing that I couldn't resist him when we danced. "What's wrong," he asked petulantly, as he tried to kiss me.

Not knowing any other way to say it, I blurted out, "I'm pregnant." I watched as his face went white and he sat down with a thud on the ground. After several minutes, he got up without another word and started walking toward my house. Hopefully, I trotted alongside him, thinking that he would ask my parents to marry me. At the gate he turned away with a muffled, "See you later."

Reassuring myself that it would take him a few days to get used to the idea, I comforted myself by daydreaming about our wedding. My dreams came crashing down the next day when Dane was not in school. *Where could he be*, I wondered. My question was answered when I overheard two girls from town gossiping that Dane wouldn't be back because he had been sent to live with his sick grandmother.

The news hit me like a blow to the gut. I ran outside and retched into the bushes. Wiping my mouth and straightening my back, I realized that I was going to have to come up with another plan. In my town, in my family, and in my church, a girl just didn't get pregnant before marriage. As I walked back into the schoolroom, I paused and looked around at the boys, most of whom had quit paying attention to me when I became Dane's girl. At that moment, Zeb turned around to look at me and gave me a big grin. Plain and raw-boned Zeb was not someone I would have normally picked, but he was a hard worker and had a gentle nature, so I gave him a brilliant smile. Blushing, he ducked his head and turned back around. I sighed and thought, *Okay...Zeb it will be.*

It didn't take long for me to have Zeb eating out of my hands. By our second week together, he had asked me to marry him. I wanted to say yes immediately, but my Christian conscience wouldn't let me agree without telling him the truth. He listened quietly and then told me that he would love me forever, and he would love my baby, too. Relieved, I made plans for a quick marriage.

Little Stella was born seven months later. She was a chubby baby, so it was hard to pass her off as premature, but that was our story and we stuck to it. Zeb was true to his word and treated Stella like a precious jewel. At times, I thought he loved her more than I did. Every time I looked at her, I thought of Dane, and wondered what my life would be like if she had not come along. I suppose that was why I was short-tempered with her sometimes, but she could be such a tiny busy-body, always under foot and nosing into everything. That was why I was so glad to send her on that errand.

That thought brought me back to the present and I realized that I'd better check on the children. Putting up my mirror and ribbons, I stepped onto the porch to call the girls away from the creek and back to the house. About that time, I saw Stella coming down the path with a big grin on her face. *Why is she so happy*, I wondered.

Stella ran to meet me on the porch and presented me with a shiny silver tube, telling me she thought it would make a pretty necklace. Touched by her thoughtfulness and pleased that I would have a new piece of jewelry, I thanked her with a smile.

I was as excited as the girls to see how it would look, so the little ones went to fetch a hammer and nail as I placed the tube on the kitchen table. Swinging that hammer was the last thing I remember.

When I awoke, I was in a hospital bed with my hand swathed in bandages and a head that ached with every heartbeat. They told me the shiny tube was a blasting cap and that the explosion had damaged my hand beyond repair.

"You mean I don't have a hand anymore," I asked quietly. No answer. "Tell me, is my hand gone?" I asked, more loudly this time. Still no answer — but the looks on their faces told me what I needed to know. "NOOOO...," I screamed. I'm not proud of how I reacted after that; the nurse eventually had to sedate me to keep me from tearing off the bandages.

When I awoke again, the dull thud of grief woke with me. I held my arms out in front of me and took a good look. "Ugly," I said savagely. To me, there was no worse insult. "Ugly and useless! Who will love you now," I whispered, and turned my face to the pillow and cried.

The next time I awoke, it occurred to me that I hadn't even asked about my children. I berated myself, *What kind of mother are you?* I was relieved when Zeb told me that they were fine and staying with the Fryes. When he left, dark thoughts began to coil in my mind like a pack of coyotes circling their prey.

"Stella..." I thought, "...it's her fault. She's the one that gave me that tube. It was her idea to make a necklace!" Anger rose up inside me and I did the unthinkable...I wished that she had never been born. She was born out of sorrow, and sorrow she had caused. Part of me knew that I was wrong, but grief and anger had swallowed me like a tidal wave. For three more days, I cried and moaned and cursed the day Stella was born. I even cursed God, although I did so under my breath because the fear of God had been instilled in me since birth.

The fourth day, instead of cursing God, I began to pray. I prayed all day and then I prayed all night. I knew I needed help, spiritual help. The fifth day, I awoke with peace instead of despair. During the sixth day, I began to think of the future and how I would manage with just one hand. The seventh day, I thought of Stella...my sweet, nosy little girl...my firstborn. It was then that I let go of the anger and blame. Stella should never be made to feel like she was at fault. It was a horrible, stupid accident and no one was to blame.

The eighth day, Zeb came to take me home. I was weak and I was scared. How was a once beautiful woman going to deal with being mutilated and scarred? Would Zeb continue to love this maimed woman? How was I going to manage a household of four children with just one hand?

Zeb gently placed his arm around me and guided me to the door, whispering encouragement all the way. He settled me in my rocker, tucking a quilt around my legs, and went to get the children. I drank in the quietness like an elixir, allowing my mind to rest from the frantic worry that had been dogging me.

Three little girls came bursting in the room, shattering the calm with their exuberant energy. Stella, the only one old enough to understand what had happened to our family, fell at my feet begging for forgiveness. I had dug myself into the quietness so deeply that I couldn't immediately respond. As I gradually roused from my languor, I reached out and placed my hand on Stella's head, reminding myself that she was not to blame. Looking down, I saw guilt and torment written all over her little face, still shiny from her tears. Love for my daughter flooded my heart, and for the first time, I felt my spine stiffen with resolve. I whispered to myself, "I will learn to live with just one hand. I will diaper my babies and I will cook their meals. I will dance and I will sing. And I will be beautiful again!"

I began to cry.

Pounding Footsteps

Linda Hudson Hoagland

Keys in hand, Samantha exited the elevator and walked swiftly through the deserted, dim parking garage. Suddenly, she heard footsteps running toward her from behind. Samantha turned around as she dug the pepper spray out of her coat pocket. She didn't know who was following her, but she was afraid he wasn't there to exchange pleasant greetings. She readied the pepper spray for use as she glanced in the direction of the pounding footsteps.

"Samantha, stop! You have a phone call. He said it is an emergency," shouted Arthur Conlin, a co-worker.

Samantha covered the pepper spray container with its plastic cap and shoved it back into her coat pocket. "Did he give you his name?"

"He said he is with the Stillwell Police Department, but I didn't get his name," said Arthur.

Samantha walked back to the elevator. She needed to return to her office to answer the phone in privacy. Arthur must have gone on home because he didn't board the elevator with her. As the doors closed she stared straight ahead, trying to figure out why the police would be calling her at work.

As soon as the doors opened, she walk-ran down the hall to reach her office. She pushed the button for the only flashing light on the telephone.

"Hello," she said breathlessly into the receiver.

There was a pause. She knew someone was listening on the other end.

"Hello, is this the police department," she asked in a calmer voice. Click.

"Hello, are you there?"

The dial tone blared in her ear as the line disconnected.

"What the heck," Samantha said as she slammed the receiver onto its cradle. She looked around to see if anyone saw her or was within earshot. She saw no one. *How odd*, she thought. There was usually someone there even if it was only the cleaning lady.

Her phone slamming temper tantrum had helped her relieve the built-up tension. She felt calm enough to try to leave again. Except this time, she was not going to hear pounding footsteps, she hoped.

Again, she boarded the elevator for her ride to the parking garage. As soon as the doors opened, she had the feeling of pending doom. The hair on the back of her neck stood up and a tingle of fear raced down her spine.

"Stop it, Samantha," she scolded herself in a whisper. "You are going to your car and you will be fine."

She glanced at her car and saw that it was parked between the only two other cars in the parking garage on this level. She did not recognize either car as an icy finger of fear jabbed her center chest. She walked closer. She saw no one sitting in the two cars next to hers, so the only hurdle facing her, she thought, was crawling into her car.

She placed her hand in her coat pocket and wrapped her fingers around the pepper spray. She used her thumb to push off the cap. She wanted to be totally ready for whomever or whatever was lying in wait. She had thrown the strap of her handbag over her shoulder, so her left hand would be able to operate the remote door lock. She kept her right hand filled with the pepper spray can inside her coat pocket.

She wanted to run, but if she did she would be more vulnerable to attack. She continued at a steady pace, turning her head from side to side checking out her desolate surroundings.

"Where is everybody," she mumbled. Even though it was past time for all the classified people to go home, most of the salaried personnel left at a slower pace.

"They just parked on a different level. That's all," she said aloud. She was trying to reinforce her backbone because it was starting to crumble. She knew that the walk to her car wasn't very long, but her fear had her convinced it was hundreds of feet further than it really was.

When she pressed the remote button to unlock her car, her headlights flashed and the momentary brightness blinded her. That was all it took.

Something came crashing down on her head and she went out like a burned out light bulb. When she forced herself back into her world, she realized she was in the backseat of her own car, and it was moving.

She moved her head a bit to see if she would have any pain. She did. It was excruciating.

"She's waking up," said a gruff sounding voice. "Want me to hit her again?"

"No, please, don't hit me," begged Samantha as she winced from the pain. Even moving her mouth to talk caused enormous pain.

"Leave her alone. We don't want her dead yet," said a female voice.

"Who are you? Why are you doing this," Samantha said painfully.

"For money; why do you think," snarled the gruff man.

"I don't have any money," said Samantha as she tried to ignore the pain.

"Your boss does," said the female voice.

The more the female talked, the more familiar her voice sounded to Samantha. She needed to keep the female talking.

"My boss isn't rich," Samantha said weakly.

"The firm has money, as does his stuck-up family," said the female.

"You're going to have to shut up or I will shoot you right now," said the man.

Samantha took him at his word and asked no more questions.

The woman, her voice, Samantha felt she knew who it was. She had to focus on it and try to remember but that was so hard to do with the pain. She wanted to touch the area where all of the pain was radiating from, but she discovered her hands and feet were zip tied and there was no hope of breaking free in her weakened condition. She was surprised that they hadn't taped her mouth. Maybe they thought she wouldn't wake up until they got her to where they were taking her.

Where am I going? That question passed through her mind before she lost consciousness again.

It didn't hurt when she wasn't awake.

Maybe that's where I need to stay, was the thought that filled her head when she started climbing out of the deep hole of darkness. She opened her eyes one at a time to find out if she was still in her car. She felt no motion, so she thought she had been moved from the vehicle. She must be in a dark room, maybe a garage, because it smelled oily and dirty.

I'm in the trunk of a car. It's not my car. My car trunk is clean and carpeted. Where am I?

She tried to move but she felt the zip ties cutting into her skin. She wanted to scream.

They taped my mouth.

She tried kicking her feet. She heard some movement outside of her place of captivity.

Maybe if I made some noise someone will help me.

The only noise coming from her mouth were indecipherable grunts. She tried to kick at her surroundings again, but her zip tied legs weren't making a loud enough noise.

I'm going to die in this nasty, old car trunk.

Out she went again. The pain in her head had made staying conscious and alert impossible. When she woke up, Arthur was standing over her.

"I've called an ambulance, Samantha. It will be here soon," he said in gentle, soothing tones.

She put her untied hand up to her mouth and discovered the tape had been removed. "How did you find me," she barely whispered.

"I followed them. I called the police and told them you had been kidnapped, and I continued following you until they finally stopped. They carried you from your car and put you in this car trunk in the Jackson Junkyard. After they left, I sneaked in and used a crowbar to pry open the trunk, and all the while, I was praying that you were still alive. Thank God you were and are still alive. I hear the ambulance coming now, as well as the police. You are safe, Samantha," explained Arthur.

"Thank you," she whispered as the EMT's placed her on a cot to be taken to the hospital.

The police questioned her about what had happened. She told them Arthur seemed to know more about it than she did. She was unconscious much of the time. She also told them that the female's voice was familiar to her. She knew she had heard it somewhere.

After the police left, she laid in the hospital bed and pondered the experience. Something was seriously wrong with all of this.

Why was Arthur so conveniently the hero? He had left before I did. He wouldn't have known I was taken away in my own car.

She was unconscious again. She knew nothing about what was taking place.

When she woke up again she was in ICU. It seemed that she had a seizure triggered by the head injury she received when the man hit her over the head. When her mind cleared up, she realized she knew who the female was that had been driving the car.

It was Arthur's wife, Melissa.

"Could you call Detective Martin at the police department and ask him to stop in to see me," she asked the ICU nurse.

"Do you feel up to it," asked the nurse.

"Yes ma'am. I really need to speak with him before I fade out again," Samantha explained.

Detective Martin arrived within an hour of receiving the summons. "What is it you need to tell me? Did you remember something?"

"Yes, sir. I figured out whom the female driver was. It was Arthur Conlin's wife, Melissa."

"Are you sure?"

"As sure as I can be after having my head cracked open," Samantha answered.

"Is there anything else," asked the detective.

"I think the man was her brother. I only saw him once before in passing, but I'm pretty sure it was him. I think his name is Jack. I don't know his last name," Samantha added.

"Do you think Arthur had anything to do with the kidnapping?" asked the detective.

"No sir. I think he knew about it. That's why he knew what to do to save me. If it hadn't been for Arthur, I'm sure I would be dead by now."

"We will check this out and get back to you as soon as possible. In the meantime, I'm going to keep a police officer posted outside of ICU. I don't want anything else happening to you."

"Thank you," said Samantha as she watched the detective leave her bedside.

She was starting to fade out again when someone entered her area. The only visitor she had been expecting was the detective, and he had already come and gone. She was fighting to keep herself alert but her eyelids kept falling.

She managed to open one eye to see that there was a man standing next to her with a syringe in his hand. She pressed the call button that was located on the inside panel of the bed rail.

The man was positioned to insert the contents of the syringe into the IV tube that was forcing medication into her aching body.

"Who are you?" demanded the ICU nurse.

"I'm Samantha's brother," he said. He had been startled by the nurse's appearance and was not able to finish the injection.

"You need to leave. We have specific times for family members to visit the ICU. You will need to come back," she instructed.

The man stepped out of the ICU area, walked to the door, and was stopped by the tardy police officer standing at the ready.

Samantha was the only patient in ICU at that time, so the police officer wanted to know what the man was doing there.

"I came to see my sister, Samantha," he mumbled.

"What is your name," the police officer asked.

"Jack Jenson," he mumbled.

"Mr. Jenson, you are under arrest for the kidnap of Samantha Thomas," he said as he forced Jack Jenson to turn by grabbing his arm and wrenching it behind him so he could handcuff him. "We already have your sister in custody."

The police officer called for backup to transfer Jack Jenson to the police station. He asked the ICU nurse to check on me to make sure I was all right. At least, that's what they told me happened because I was faded out again.

It took several weeks, but the trips into unconsciousness finally came to an end.

When I returned to work, I was welcomed back like a long, lost family member.

Melissa Conlin and Jack Jenson went to prison for kidnap, attempted murder, extortion, and many other sundry charges. It was my hope that they would never get out of prison.

Arthur was gone. I didn't know where he went. He was never charged with a crime. I saw to that, because he did save my life.

Sarah-Hannah

Betty Kossick

Savannah, Georgia is where Sarah-Hannah drew her first breath. Her French ancestors settled there, having fled the French Revolution in the late 1700's. Her momma (maman), Lindy Sue, birthed her on a blistering-hot summer evening, with the fragrance of honeysuckle in the air, and Sarah-Hannah's poppa (pere) sweating as much as Lindy Sue. Trevor Judge could barely stand the cries emitting from his beloved wife, he felt weak as he sat by her side with her fingernails pricking his palm as she gripped him with every birth pain.

After waiting 15 years for a baby, they finally held this child of their own. They felt overjoyed that their prayers were heard. Sarah-Hannah no sooner cried her first than her pere offered thanks to God for the red, squirming baby. He adored her from first sight.

Sarah-Hannah's hyphenated name was her maman's making. She wanted their daughter to be named after both her mother and Trevor's mother. And she didn't want one name preferred over the other. Trevor agreed but felt it was a bit fancy, choosing to call her Annie, just as his mother was called.

Lindy Sue thought it sweet of her husband, but told him, "Trevor, I shall call her Sarah-Hannah." As it turned out, no one else ever called Sarah-Hannah Annie except her pere, so she became "Annie" to him alone.

61

Trevor never considered any task of his wife's as being simply woman's work. Though he was a respected attorney, a partner with one of Savannah's renowned legal firms, when he came home at work day's end, he always asked his Lindy Sue, "What may I do to help you this evening?"

Her usual reply being, "Not a thing, lovey, except help me cleanup after supper." All those in their circle of friends were aware of the couple's devotion to each other and to Sarah-Hannah.

Sarah-Hannah's maman didn't work beyond the home after her child's birth. She'd been educated at the best music schools in the area, trained as a pianist, and found much pleasure in teaching children at the Chastain Conservatory of Music. However, after becoming a mother at age 40, she and Trevor decided she'd be a stay-at-home mom. She acquired a reputation as a dedicated volunteer at church and in the Savannah community at large. Her special interest included helping abused women and children.

Sarah-Hannah followed in her mother's footsteps. She often told her maman, "It makes me happy to help other people."

However, Sarah-Hannah held a longing desire that would take her away from Savannah, which leads us to discover her story:

Debutante Days

At age 16, Sarah-Hannah was one of the best known young women of Savannah's debutante events. Those who sponsored such events always hoped for her participation, though her reputation as a top scholar and as an avid volunteer who looked after the needs of the abused, didn't seem to fit the debutante role. Nothing about her life seemed self-indulgent, yet the gowns she wore were always the eye-catchers — made by her favorite designer, her maman. And she always seemed at ease in any setting. Stalwarts in the community, the Judge family were beloved by community leaders and the poorest-of-the-poor alike. As well, Sarah-Hannah early-on corralled a circle of beaus.

Sarah-Hannah often went to the docks with her best friend, Caroline LeDuc, to watch the ships sailing off to the Atlantic with their crew and passengers. She held an affinity for the story of Florence Martus, known as, "the waving girl," of whom so many residents, travelers, and sailors wove romantic tales about.

Caroline told her often, "I know that you will sail off one of these days, and I will wave to you just as Florence did to all those people."

Florence was a real person, who took it upon herself to greet ships at the city's port from 1887–1931. When she was 19, she started her famous, daily waving to ships as they entered port. Sailors and travelers took the lore to far-off ports. Though many claimed that she awaited a sweetheart to return, Sarah-Hannah knew Florence's reason for the waving held no romantic trappings because she'd read an interview about Florence, who lived with her brother, the lighthouse keeper on Elba Island, "I was young, and it was sort of lonely living on the Island for a girl, so I started to wave to the ships which passed. They would return the greeting and sometimes salute. Gradually they came to watch for my wave from the shore. We had many friends on the tugboats and among the bar pilots." A statue of Florence, who never married, was commissioned as an honor to her faithful years of greeting ships sailing in or leaving the Atlantic harbor at Savannah.

However, for Sarah-Hannah, her reason for the dockside visits was, as her friend Caroline ascertained, her long-held desire to travel abroad. Before her mother married Trevor, Lindy Sue spent a year in Paris. Lindy Sue desired to expand her talent as a pianist and was advised that Paris was "the place" to study. She often told her daughter about "the sweet year of my young womanhood." Lindy Sue also spoke lovingly about her beloved mentor, Madame Beatrice Boucher. Now Sarah-Hannah held the same longing — to study abroad.

Trevor didn't appreciate his Annie's want to study abroad, "Savannah offers enough excellent teaching of the piano," he insisted, though he was aware of the antebellum carryover for young women to study piano, whether they be talented or not, in order to attract a good husband. Many husbands of the 1950's enjoyed ending their work day sitting back in an easy chair and listening to their wives play soothing tunes. And a young woman entertaining her beau with genteel music at the piano was considered safe wooing. Even though Lindy Sue had taught Sarah-Hannah herself, she didn't seem sympathetic to her daughter's want to study abroad, even though she'd enjoyed her experience under Madame Boucher's tutelage.

Then on the evening of her 21st birthday, Sarah-Hannah requested a "family meeting" after her parents presented her with a birthday celebration, and all the merry-makers left. "Pere, Maman, I've been attending the university for two years and I'm not really sure of what I want to do with my life, except that my happiest moments are at the piano. Maman you've been a successful piano teacher, and I feel perhaps that I can be too. Also, I might as well tell you that Chandler proposed to me tonight and I did not accept. My heart ached for him, but I'm not ready for marriage. I don't feel that he is either. He has three years yet to finish his engineering studies, and I think he should do that before he thinks about taking on a wife. I admire him greatly and have found him a dear friend, but am I in love with him? I don't think so. That's why he took his leave early tonight. I suppose that I broke his heart. I yearn to do what you did, Maman, — go to Paris to study. I'm asking for your blessing to go."

Lindy Sue spoke softly, "Paris gave me the wherewithal that I needed to be the music teacher I aspired to be. With my French heritage and study of the language, I knew enough to get me through living alone abroad — and I know that you can too. You've mastered the language better than I — and you're far more independent."

"My sweet Annie, your Maman is right. But I must say that you turned down a fine young man in Chandler Whittaker. I'm sure that he would be willing to wait for you. He obviously loves you."

"Yes, Pere, he's a dear, but I don't love him as a sweetheart. I cherish him as a friend. He's fun to be with and I consider him as one of my best friends. He'll provide someone with a good life, someone whom will love him as he needs to be loved."

Sarah-Hannah reached out her arms to her parents and embraced them both together, with a request, "Let's plan this as a team, could we make a holiday of it when I leave — you go with me to help me settle into an apartment? I'm not expecting you to finance this endeavor. You know that when Grandmaman passed, she left me a sizeable gift for my education. Pere, you've never been to France, so this can be your opportunity. That way we won't all be sobbing as we part company for a while. And Maman, we know that Madame Boucher's son, Paul-Jean, inherited her studio when she passed, and he's made such a fine reputation in French music circles, so wouldn't he be the best bet for me to seek out for advanced tutoring?"

Lindy Sue smiled. "I'm convinced, Sarah-Hannah."

"Me, too, Annie," her pere said.

"It will be wonderful to see Paris again," her maman sighed.

Southern-American Belle in Paris

Regardless of Sarah-Hannah's determination not to weep when her parents set sail back to America, she did — and so did they. Just a few weeks prior, they'd celebrated her twenty-first birthday back in Savannah. She was born on July 14, 1931 (she loved her birth-date because it's Bastille Day (1799), a day that marked a turn in the French Revolution and eventually brought her relatives to America, first to South Carolina, then to Georgia). Now it was September 1, 1952 and here she was in France. She felt brave and scared, and perhaps a bit wild at the same time. Yet her desire to develop her musical skills and to experience the land of her forebearers buoyed her on.

During the past three weeks, she'd already met several new friends and felt comfortable in the little village outside Paris where she'd stay for the next two years. Claude and Juliette LeBlanc, longtime friends of Paul-Jean Boucher as well as her maman, Lindy Sue, insisted that Sarah-Hannah occupy the small guest house adjacent to their home. She could use their piano for practice.

Juliette reminded Sarah-Hannah, "I, too, studied with Madam Beatrice, five years before your mother came to study, though my studies weren't for professional reasons, but only to acquaint myself with the beauty of the art. My parents felt it the proper thing for a young woman to do. The lessons were a fine gift because I met another student of hers, Claude — and love bloomed; now as horticulturists we create blooms together in our gardens."

"Oh, how I love the LeBlancs and their fairy-like gardens," Sarah-Hannah wrote to her parents a month after they left. "I feel so peaceful here. I believe that every flower, every plant, and every tree they chose for this space is blessed. Of course, they being horticulturists, most of what they've planted are their own developed hybrids. And do you know that they pray about their work? The roses are especially to my liking. I even talk to the flowers, because I'm told it helps them to grow more beautiful. True or not, I find my conversation among them my special-happy time."

By early springtime, Sarah-Hannah settled well into her studies with Paul-Jean. She found him a taskmaster who required her best but with an unending, kind countenance. He told her that her mother, Lindy Sue, who studied under his mother's wings, had tutored her well and she passed on excellent skills to Sarah-Hannah. He found her like a sponge in tackling the more advanced musical arrangements. With constant encouragement, her life became immersed with the knowledge of piano. Paul-Jean felt that she'd be ready for her first recital at the Easter season; thus, her emphasis was in preparing for the music she wanted to perform at the Academie Boucher LaFrance.

Good Friday, April 14, 1953 arrived and Sarah-Hannah looked forward to the recital. All those participating in the recital would be presenting unique arrangements of spiritually embedded music for the season. Her parents flew to Paris via Air France for the event. As a tradition set with Madame Boucher and Academie Boucher LaFrance, and now with her son Paul-Jean, the mayor (maire) of the village, Daniel LeBrun in this case, would moderate the event.

As a surprise they brought along Sarah-Hannah's beloved friend Caroline. The two friends fell into a tight embrace, "Caroline, how I've missed you!"

"Life's been so different without your friendship to surround me, Sarah-Hannah," Caroline called out. "I felt beside myself with joy when your parents asked me to come along. Such a delightful engagement gift."

"Engagement? How wonderful! When did this happen? Your letters never revealed anything about marriage. Who is the lucky fellow?"

"Brace yourself, Sarah-Hannah. It's — it's Chandler!"

"Chandler?! Oh, my. Whatever happened to Billy Ray? I figured he would be the one."

"He decided to move to Alaska. He loves piloting and decided to become a bush pilot. He did ask me to marry him before he left, but I knew his adventurous spirt and my homebody one weren't going to make a good fit. I'd felt it for a while. He did, too, I think. We parted kindly."

"Well, you and Chandler are marrying yourselves good ones. I'm so happy for you; my two best friends marrying each other. How wonderful. When did this romance start?"

"Just a few months ago at a Christmas party that Polly Martin held at her home. We got to talking about you — and then our conversation led to other subjects, and we discovered that we had a mutual interest in so many things. He asked me to attend Christmas Eve church services with him, and we've been a thing since. I love him, Sarah-Hannah — and I know that though he did ask for your hand in marriage, he's over you and loves me now."

"Of course! When will the wedding be?"

"Chandler will be out of the country in South America, working on an internship for four months as a part of his studies, so we decided for next summer, when Georgia roses are in full bloom for a garden wedding."

Sarah-Hannah hugged her friend close, "We've got a double reason to celebrate after the recital, don't we, Caroline?"

Three days later...

"H-e-l-l-o Sarah-Hannah, are you ready? We've got to leave for the recital," called Juliette.

"Pere, Maman, Caroline, see you in about hour! I've got butterflies, but I'm thrilled about the recital."

Juliette and Sarah-Hannah both chatted non-stop on the way to the Academie. Sarah-Hannah's excitement seemed like a percolating coffee pot. She bounced out of the taxi as they arrived — and just moments later Juliette screamed, "No, no!" as she saw Sarah-Hannah fall in her hurry. She dropped to her knees to help.

"Juliette, the pain is terrible, I think I've broken my ankle. Look my foot's twisted out!" A siren already wailed, someone else saw and called an ambulance. Just as it arrived, Paul-Jean ran out of the Academie, "Paul-Jean, I'm so sorry. In my rush I stumbled and fell, I think my ankle is broken."

"Yes, it looks like it. Don't worry about the recital; the other performers are here. The recital will go on. When your time is announced for performance, I will ask the entire audience to pray for you."

Through painful tears, Sarah-Hannah waved a courageous adieu, as the ambulance drove off, with Juliette by her side.

Phillipe Beauregard

The next morning, when Sarah-Hannah awoke, her parents were already at her bedside, along with Caroline. Immediately, she started apologizing for her fall, "I've made a mess out of a time for celebration, didn't I? What must Paul-Jean think of me?"

"Annie, Paul-Jean loves you like a daughter. He made such a plea for prayer for you during the recital that every eye was wet," Trevor assured his daughter.

Lindy Sue squeezed Sarah-Hannah's hand — and it made her think of the night of her daughter's birth, when she squeezed Trevor's hand in birth pain, "We're just grateful that it wasn't worse."

Caroline came alongside the bed and caressed her friend's face, "You'll perform in the next recital — and you'll steal the show."

While everyone was trying to reassure Sarah-Hannah, the orthopedic surgeon walked into the hospital room, and called out in English woven with a heavy French accent, "Mademoiselle Judge may I come in? I'm Dr. Durand, and this is Phillipe Beauregard, one of our finest physical therapists. And how are you doing this morning, Mademoiselle? I hear that you missed your opportunity to do, what is it you Americans say? "Wow them" at the Academie yesterday. I'm so sorry. But that broken ankle will heal with expert therapy; you'll be as good as new — and soon ready for the next recital. When you're chosen to present in a recital at the Acadamie, you are excellent.

"When I learned that you are an American, studying here in France, I knew that Phillippe would best for your recuperation because he studied physical therapy in the United States, and he speaks fluent English. You're in good hands with Phillipe. Are you agreeable?"

Sarah-Hannah replied, "Thank you for putting my ankle together again and for your consideration about what is best for my therapy."

"My honor to help you, Mademoiselle, You'll be wearing a cast for a few weeks, then start your therapy with Phillipe. The better you cooperate with your therapy, the sooner you'll heal, though you need to know that complete recovery may take up to a year, even though you'll be able to drive a car and engage in simple exercise within a few weeks." Dr. Durand turned to Phillipe, "Young man, you should especially enjoy this patient, she's not only talented but she's a pretty one."

Sarah-Hannah's face flushed.

"Literally, I'll be helping you get back on your feet," Phillipe assured her, as he turned and shook hands with Trevor and greeted both Lindy Sue and Caroline. Dr. Durand did the same. Sarah-Hannah watched them as they departed, Phillipe glancing back and casting a broad smile toward her.

Three months later...July 14, 1953

"It seems like forever since I broke my ankle, Dr. Durand, but here I am done with my physical therapy, back to normal living, and this evening I'll finally present my recital at the Academie — on Bastille Day and it's my twenty-second birthday! I'm so glad that you and Phillipe can attend. Silly Phillipe told me that he's taking me to dinner at the Francois Café, and personally escorting me to be sure that I don't fall again. Does that mean that he thinks I'm a klutz?"

Dr. Durand tossed his head back as he guffawed, "Hardly, Mademoiselle, the man is madly in love with you. He wants to protect you."

With a nervous laugh, Sarah-Hannah admitted to Dr. Durand that it was worth breaking her ankle, and missing the initial piano recital, to find her Prince Charming. "Thank you for the part you played in our romance. Can you imagine, that he asked me for a date when I was still wearing the cast?"

Dr. Durand bows, "And this is your last check-up with me; you're dismissed from my care. But I'll be sitting with the audience tonight, proud of my patient."

At Café Francois

"Are you nervous about the recital, Sarah-Hannah?"

"A bit, Phillipe, yet thrilled about it. Actually, I expect it to be the high-light of today. After all it's my birthday and France's cherished holiday,

69

Bastille Day; I was dismissed from Dr. Durand's care, and am at dinner with the dearest man in the world, then the recital. My parents and Caroline are here again for it all. What could best it all?"

"My love, I hope my birthday gift does." Phillipe opened a small, pink, velvet box, "Sarah-Hannah, I love you with all my heart, will you marry me?"

With her green eyes glistening, she softly replied, "Yes, yes! I love you, Phillipe," as he slipped a ring on her finger. "I'm the happiest woman in the world."

"I hope that you don't care, Sarah-Hannah, but I asked your Pere for his permission to ask you. He told me with a catch in his throat that he adored you from his first sight of you, and I told him it was the same for me when I first saw you in the hospital with your ankle cast. And I told him more that I must tell you; I've decided to move to the United States to work in Atlanta. You won't have to leave Georgia. As you know, my sister Suzanne has been after me to move there where she and Andre live. With our parents gone, there's nothing to tie me here permanently — and you and I can return to France for vacations. What do you think?"

"As I said, I'm the happiest woman in the world, but I would have stayed with you here in France because I know you love your homeland. I'd be happy to live anywhere as Mrs. Phillipe Beauregard. I want us to be the happiest ever-after couple ever!"

About the Authors

Jan Howery
"Right or Wrong"

Jan Howery, a native a Southwest Virginia, writes with an Appalachian influence. Her many writings includes a short story, "The Daisy Flower Garden," featured in the book *Broken Petals*, and "The Devil Behind the Barn," featured in the book *These Haunted Hills*. Other writings include fashion and health columns for the magazines, *Voice Magazine for Women* and *Modern Day Appalachian Woman* magazine.

Linda Hudson Hoagland
"Set Up"

"Just Drive"

"Pounding Footsteps"

Linda Hudson Hoagland is the author of fiction, nonfiction, short stories, poetry, and stage plays. Hoagland has won numerous awards for her work, including first place for the Pearl S. Buck Award for Social Change and the Sherwood Anderson Short Story Contest.

Betty Kossick
"Sarah-Hannah"

As of 2018, Betty Kossick, 87, remains a versatile freelance writer/journalist/poet with 47 years of published works in newspapers and magazines. With "Wild Daisies," she now is a part of 86 books, three of which are her solo books. "Pleasure still comes with every assignment, idea, and publication." Her work has received awards, especially in the realm of social issues.

Lori C. Byington
"Gumption"

Lori C. Byington lives in Bristol, TN with her husband, Mark, son, Lee, and two dogs. She is the Assistant Professor of English at King University, where she teaches Freshman Composition and Research and Writing. In her free time, Lori enjoys time with her family, teaching, snow skiing with her son, riding her horse, writing, and baking and cooking.

Victoria Fletcher
"Second Chances"

Victoria Fletcher has lived all her life in Damascus, VA. She has published 19 books, and also runs a publishing business, Hoot Books Publishing. She is president of the Appalachian Authors Guild, chair of the Appalachian Heritage Writers Symposium, a member of the Lost State Writers Guild, and a member of the Damascus Writers Guild. She works for First Baptist Church of Damascus, VA where she is also a member.

Cheryl Livingston
"Pretty Ribbons"

Cheryl Livingston grew up in the mountains of North Carolina, listening to tales of family members who had lived in the shadow of the Cranberry Ore Mine. She now lives in Tennessee, where she and her husband cut, push, and prod pieces of colored glass into completed works of stained glass art. Cheryl recently published a children's book, *The Crayon (W)Rapper.*

Julia Parsell
"Bess's Story"

Julia Parsell is a certified holistic health coach, owner and developer of Java J's (2002-2012) and former home educator. She lives happily married in Western North Carolina; writing is her passion along with her seven grandchildren. She also loves herbology, trail blazing and creating recipes for healthy living. Visit her at juliaparsell.com

Jan-Carol Publishing, Inc

"every story needs a book"

LITTLE CREEK BOOKS
MOUNTAIN GIRL PRESS
EXPRESS EDITIONS
DIGISTYLE
ROSEHEART
BROKEN CROW RIDGE

JanCarolPublishing.com